THE FAREWELL PARTY

Milan Kundera was born in 1929 in Czechoslovakia and since
1975 has been living in France.

MILAN KUNDERA

The Farewell Party

Translated by
Peter Kussi

faber and faber
LONDON · BOSTON

First published in Great Britain in 1977 by
John Murray (Publishers) Limited
50 Albemarle Street London W1X 4BD
This paperback edition first published in 1993
by Faber and Faber Limited
3 Queen Square London WC1N 3AU

Printed in England by Clays Ltd, St Ives plc

There was no Czech edition of this book but
there was a French translation entitled *La
Valse Aux Adieux* © Editions Gallimard (1976)

A CIP record for this book is
available from the British Library

ISBN 0-571-16887-6

2 4 6 8 10 9 7 5 3 1

Contents

First Day

1

Autumn had arrived. In the lovely valley trees were turning yellow, red, brown, and the small health-resort town seemed to be surrounded by flames. Women were strolling under the colonnades of the spa, now and again pausing to lean over the spouting springs. These were childless women who had come to the spa in the hope of gaining fertility.

There was a handful of men among the patients, too, for in addition to its gynecologic wonders a cure at the spa was supposedly beneficial for heart ailments. All the same, females outnumbered males nine to one—an infuriating ratio for a young nurse like Ruzena, ministering all day to the needs of sterile matrons.

Ruzena had been born in the resort town, both of her parents still lived there, and she wondered whether she would ever manage to escape from that teeming nest of women.

It was Monday afternoon, near the end of her shift. Just the last few plump biddies to be wrapped up in sheets, bedded down, and smiled at.

"How about that phone call?" prodded Ruzena's colleagues. One was about thirty-five years old, stout, the other younger and thinner.

"Sure. Why not," answered Ruzena.

"There's nothing to be afraid of," the older nurse said reassuringly, steering Ruzena toward the back of the dressing room where the staff had their lockers, table, and telephone.

"You should really call him at his home," the thin girl said maliciously, and the three of them burst into laughter.

When their glee had subsided, Ruzena said: "I know the number of that ballroom where he rehearses. I'll call him there."

2

It was a terrifying conversation. He was alarmed the moment he recognized her voice.

He had always been afraid of women but they never believed him when he told them so, preferring to regard his confession as a gallant pleasantry.

"How are you?" he asked.

"Not too well."

"What's wrong?"

"I need to talk to you," she said with heavy pathos.

It was precisely this pathetic tone which he had been anticipating with dread for years.

"Certainly," he said in a subdued voice.

She repeated: "I really must talk to you."

"What's the trouble?"

"Something's happened since I saw you."

He could hardly speak. After a pause he said softly: "What do you mean?"

"It's been six weeks now."

He tried to control himself: "That sometimes happens. Sometimes it's a little late, that's all."

"No, this time it's the real thing."

"That's impossible. It's simply impossible. Anyway, it's not my fault, that's for sure!"

She flared up: "What do you take me for, for God's sake!"

He was afraid of her, afraid of making her angry. "Don't get me wrong, I didn't mean to insult you. Why would I want to insult you? I am only trying to say that it couldn't have been my fault. You've got nothing to worry about because I couldn't have done anything like that, it's simply physiologically impossible."

"In that case everything is perfectly all right," she said icily. "Forgive me for disturbing you."

"Oh no, please!" he said quickly, afraid that she might hang up on him. "You were quite right to phone me! Naturally I will be glad to help you. These things can be arranged, of course."

"How do you mean 'arranged'?"

He was at a loss, not daring to call the thing by its real name: "Well, you know, arranged!"

"I know what you're thinking, and you'd better get that idea right out of your head. I'd never do such a thing, they'd have to kill me first."

Terror seized him again, but he managed something of a counterattack: "If you don't want my opinion, why bother calling me? Do you want to talk this over with me or is your mind all made up?"

"I want to talk it over with you."

"All right then, I'll come out to see you."

"When?"

"I'll let you know."

"All right."

"In the meantime, take care of yourself."

"You, too."

He hung up and returned to the stage, where his band was waiting to resume rehearsal. "That's it for today, gentlemen," he said.

3

_____

She hung up the receiver, her face flushed with indignation. The way Klima had reacted to her news insulted her. Actually, she had been feeling resentful for quite some time.

They had met two months earlier, when the famous trumpeter was entertaining at the spa with his band. After the concert, there had been a party given in honor of the musicians, to which she had been invited. The trumpeter favored her over all the women present, and spent the night with her.

She had not heard a word from him since. She sent him two postcards with friendly greetings, both of which he ignored. Once, when she was visiting the capital, she telephoned him at the ballroom where he was supposed to be rehearsing. A man answered the phone, asked for her name, and said he would look for Klima. In a few minutes he came back with the news that the rehearsal was over and Mr. Trumpeter had left.

She suspected he was trying to avoid her, and her resentment of him grew with her growing suspicion that she was pregnant.

"He says it's physiologically impossible! Can you beat that? Physiologically impossible! I wonder what he'll say when the baby comes popping out!"

Her two friends nodded excitedly. The morning after her indescribable night with the famous musician, she told her colleagues all about it and the story buzzed through the steamy air of the treatment room. Ever since, the trumpeter had been the common property of the nursing staff. His picture was mounted on the wall of the staff room, and whenever his name came up they all chuckled to themselves as if he were an intimate acquaintance. And when the nurses learned that Ruzena was pregnant they were filled with a strange joy, for he had now established a tangible, long-lasting bond with them, a pledge implanted deep in Ruzena's belly.

The older nurse patted Ruzena on the back. "Now, now, dear, calm down. I have something to show you." She hurriedly leafed through a dog-eared issue of an illustrated magazine. "Here, look!" The page was taken up by a photograph of a young, attractive brunette standing on stage and holding a microphone.

Ruzena peered at the picture, trying to read her fate from that rectangle of glossy paper. "I didn't know she was so young," she said anxiously.

"Go on!" laughed her middle-aged friend. "That picture was

taken ten years ago! The two of them are the same age, you know that. She can't hold a candle to you!"

4

_____

In the course of his phone conversation with Ruzena, Klima came to realize that hers was the voice of doom he had been dreading for years. Not that he had a sound reason for believing that he had really impregnated Ruzena that fateful night (on the contrary, he was certain that her accusation was false), but he had long been anticipating this kind of news, years before he had ever met Ruzena.

He had been twenty-one when a certain infatuated blonde came up with the idea of feigning pregnancy so as to blackmail him into marriage. Those were terrible weeks; in the end he had been stricken with stomach cramps and suffered a complete collapse. Since then he had known that pregnancy was a blow that could strike at any time or place, a bolt against which no lightning rod offered any protection. The storm came heralded by a certain pathetic tone of voice over the telephone (yes, that time, too, the bad news had first struck over the phone). Ever since his youthful experience, though his affairs with women did not lack ardor, they were accompanied by feelings of anxiety, and after each liaison he waited fearfully for dire consequences. On the rational plane, he comforted himself with the thought that due to his near-pathological caution, the possibility of disaster was hardly a thousandth of one percent, but even that infinitesimal chance made him shudder.

Once, finding himself with a free evening, he called up a girl whom he had not seen for two months. As soon as she recognized his voice she exclaimed: "Darling, it's you! I was praying for you to call me! I really needed to talk to you!" She said it so breathlessly, with so much urgency, that the familiar pang of anxiety squeezed his chest, and he felt in his very soul that he was doomed.

Yet he was seized by the urge to learn the truth as quickly

as possible, so he blurted out: "Why are you speaking in such a tragic tone of voice?"

"My mother died yesterday," she answered.

He sighed with relief, but he knew that sooner or later the dreaded moment was sure to come.

5

"All right now. Out with it! What's going on?" The drummer's insistent question finally brought Klima back to his senses. He saw the worried faces of his musicians and told them what had happened. The boys put away their instruments and gathered around their leader.

The first piece of advice, offered by the eighteen-year-old guitarist, was radical: that kind of woman must be put in her place. "Tell her to go to hell. It's not your kid, and you couldn't care less. Anyway, a blood test would show soon enough who knocked her up."

Klima countered that blood tests generally proved nothing either way, so that in the end the woman's accusation still would stand.

The guitarist retorted that no actual blood test would be needed: when that type of girl is treated with firmness, she is damn careful not to create any more trouble for herself. As soon as she learns that the accused man is not a trembling milksop, she has that thing removed at her own expense. "Anyway, if she went ahead and had the kid, every last one of us would swear he'd shacked up with her. Then let 'em guess who's the real daddy!"

But Klima said: "I know I can count on all of you. But by that time I'd be dead of worry and fear. When it comes to these things I am the world's greatest coward, and I've got to have some certainty as soon as possible."

They all nodded in agreement. The guitarist's approach was sound in principle, but it was not for everybody. It was certainly not suitable for a man with weak nerves, nor for a famous and rich man for whose sake women were willing to take foolish risks. The band thus shifted to the opinion that rather than outright rejection, it was more advisable to persuade the girl to undergo an abortion. But what arguments should be employed? Three basic strategies presented themselves:

The first approach was aimed at the girl's compassionate heart. According to this plan, Klima would treat her as his most intimate friend, bare his soul to her, confide to her in all sincerity that his wife was gravely ill and would surely collapse if she were to learn that another woman was to have her husband's child. Klima, unable to bear such a calamity, morally or psychologically, would beg the nurse to take pity on him.

There was, however, a fundamental objection to this line of attack: it was folly to build an entire strategy upon something as uncertain and untested as the nurse's supposed tenderheartedness. If the girl did not happen to have a kind and compassionate heart, she would turn this weapon against him. Insulted by the undue concern the chosen father of her child was showing toward another woman, she would proceed all the more coldly and harshly.

The second method was intended to appeal to the girl's common sense: Klima would try to explain to her that he had no assurance that the child was really his, and this doubt would always linger in his mind. After all, he had spent only one night with the nurse and knew practically nothing about her. He didn't have the faintest idea what other male friends she may have had. No, he was not accusing her of deliberate deceit, but surely she could not maintain that he was the only man in her life! And even if she were to insist that this was so, where could Klima find the conviction to give him peace of mind? And would it be wise to give birth to a child whose father would always have lingering doubts about its paternity? Could Klima be expected to abandon his wife for the sake of an infant he was not even convinced was his? And certainly Ruzena would not have the heart to bring up a child destined never to meet its father?

The drawbacks to this approach were also of a fundamental nature. The bass player (the oldest man in the band) pointed out that it was even more foolish to count on a girl's common sense than on her compassion. The logic of the argument was sure to miss the mark, while the girl's heart was bound to be wounded by her beloved's mistrust. This would only strengthen her tearful stubbornness and provoke her to even more brazen determination.

There was a third possible strategy: Klima could assure the pregnant girl that he had loved her once and that he loved her still. Far from accusing her of duplicity, he would shower her with trust and tenderness. He would promise everything, including a speedy divorce from his wife, and hint at a wonderful future together. And for the sake of that future, he would ask her to terminate her pregnancy. He would explain that this was not the most opportune time for them to have a baby, and that premature parenthood would deprive them of the beautiful first years of conjugal happiness.

This line of argument lacked the one quality that the others possessed in abundance: logic. If Klima was so crazy about the nurse, why had he managed to ignore her completely for the past two months? But the bass player maintained that logic and love were incompatible, and that Klima was sure to come up with some plausible explanation. In the end, they all agreed that this third strategy was probably the best all-around approach, for it utilized the only reasonably certain element in the entire affair—the girl's affection.

6

The band broke up outside the theater, but the guitarist accompanied Klima all the way home. He was the only dissenter to the proposed plan, which seemed to him unworthy of the bandleader, his hero and idol.

"When dealing with women, bring your whip," he cited

Nietzsche, a philosopher whose other utterances were totally unknown to him.

"My dear fellow," sighed Klima, "unfortunately it's not I who has the whip hand, but that woman."

The guitarist then offered to drive to the spa, entice the nurse out on the highway, and run her over with his car. "Nobody could prove it wasn't an accident," he said.

The guitarist was the youngest member of the band; he loved Klima and Klima was moved by his words: "You're very nice," Klima told him.

The guitarist expounded on his plan with mounting enthusiasm, his cheeks aflame.

"That's awfully decent of you, but it won't work," interjected Klima.

"Why dillydally? She's a bitch!"

"No You're an awfully decent fellow. Thanks. But it won't work," said Klima, and took his leave.

When he found himself alone, Klima thought about the young fellow's plan and about the reasons he had turned it down. He was no more virtuous than the guitarist—only more timid. He feared an accusation of murder as much as one of paternity. He visualized a car running over Ruzena's body, he imagined her lying on the road in a pool of blood, and he felt a few moments of blissful relief. But he realized there was no point in lulling himself with such sweet visions. Anyway, he had a more immediate problem: tomorrow was his wife's birthday!

It was a few minutes before six, and the stores were just about to close. He dashed into the nearest flower shop and bought an enormous bouquet of roses. It occurred to him that tomorrow was sure to be a day of agony. He would have to pretend to be with his wife body and soul, he would have to hover attentively at her side, to amuse her, laugh with her, and yet in reality his thoughts would be totally concerned with the swelling belly of a distant stranger. He would chatter away merrily, but his mind would be far away, imprisoned in the dark recesses of another woman's body.

He realized that it would be beyond his endurance to spend his wife's birthday at home, and he decided not to postpone the visit to Ruzena any longer.

Of course, the prospect of such a trip was not very enticing, either. The thought of the remote spa was like a whiff of some vapid desert. He knew nobody there, except for one American who gave the impression of a rich landowner stuck in a provincial nest. After Klima's ill-fated concert, this American had been the one to entertain the band in his apartment, ply them with excellent food and drink and introduce them to all the pretty nurses. Thus he was indirectly responsible for Klima's affair with Ruzena. Oh, if only the American were still there, a man who had treated him with immense cordiality! Klima clung to this vision as if his salvation depended on it. In predicaments such as the one Klima was facing, nothing is more reassuring than the sympathetic understanding of another man.

He returned to the rehearsal hall and asked the doorman to arrange the long-distance call to Ruzena. Soon he was hearing her voice. He told her he would be coming tomorrow. He didn't say a word about the matter she had brought up earlier. He was talking to her as if they were two lovers without a care in the world.

Casually he asked: "By the way, is that wealthy American still there?"

"Yes, he is," said Ruzena.

He felt relieved, and repeated somewhat more gaily than before how much he was looking forward to seeing her. "Tell me, what are you wearing just now?" he asked.

"Why?"

This was one of his favorite tricks to play on the phone, and he had been using it successfully for years. "I want to know how you're dressed. I want to have a picture of you in my mind."

"I'm wearing a red dress."

"I'll bet red looks good on you."

"I guess so."

"And what about underneath?"

She laughed. They always laughed at that point.

"What kind of panties have you got on?"

"They're red, too."

"I can't wait to see you in them."

He hung up. It seemed to him that he had found just the right tone to use with her, and for a while he felt relieved. But only for a while. He soon realized that he was unable to get his mind off the Ruzena problem, and that any attempt to keep up small talk with his wife would likely prove an enormous strain. He stopped at the box office of a movie theater and bought two tickets for an American Western.

8

Even though Mrs. Klima's great beauty far outweighed her poor health, she was nonetheless sickly. It was her precarious health that had forced her to give up a singing career, a career which had led her into the arms of the man who was to become her husband.

After illness struck, the beautiful young woman so accustomed to admiration suddenly found herself in a dreary world reeking of boredom and disinfectant, a world oceans away from the glittering one she and her husband had been sharing.

Klima sympathized. Seeing her sorrowful face broke his heart, and from his own glamorous world he tried to reach out to her with compassion (across those imaginary oceans). Kamila soon came to realize that her sorrow contained an unsuspected power to attract and to move. Not surprisingly, she began to exploit this accidentally discovered advantage (perhaps unconsciously, but no less frequently). After all, it was only when she saw him gazing into her pained face that she could be reasonably sure his mind was on no other woman.

This beautiful lady was afraid of women, and saw them everywhere. She never missed a single one. She knew how to detect them from the tone of Klima's voice when he greeted her at the door and even from the smell of his clothes. Recently she had found on his desk a scrap of torn newspaper on which a date had been jotted down in his handwriting. Naturally, this could refer to any number of possible appointments, such as a concert rehearsal or a meeting with an agent, but for an entire month she thought of nothing but the identity of the woman Klima was about to meet on that date, and for an entire month she did not get a good night's sleep.

If she was so terrified by the treacherous world of women, could she not find solace in the world of men?

Hardly. Jealousy throws a remarkably narrow spotlight on one single man, while all other males merge into a dark mass in the background. Mrs. Klima, hypnotized by this tormenting spotlight, was blind to all men in the world but one: her husband.

Now she heard a key turning and the man was standing in the door, holding a bouquet of roses.

Her first reaction was joy, but doubts set in at once: Why was he bringing flowers now, when her birthday was not till the next day? What was going on?

"You won't be here tomorrow?" she greeted him.

9

His bringing roses on the eve of her birthday, of course, did not necessarily mean that he would not be home the next day. But her outstretched antennae, eternally watchful, eternally jealous, were capable of detecting her husband's secret plans far in advance.

Whenever Klima became aware of these terrible antennae focused on him, spying on him, stripping him bare, he was seized by an overwhelming sense of fatigue. He hated those antennae, and he was convinced that if his marriage was threatened by anything, it was those damned quivering feelers. He was always certain (with a belligerently clear conscience) that any deception he may have practiced on his wife had been motivated solely by his desire to shelter her and to keep her from needless worry, and he was convinced that his wife's suffering was of her own doing.

He glanced at her face, which emanated suspicion, gloom, and ill humor. He felt like tossing the bouquet on the floor, but he controlled himself. He knew that in the next few days his self-control would have to meet far sterner tests.

"You don't mind that I am a bit early with the flowers?" he said. His wife noticed the irritation in his voice. She shook her head and began to fill a vase with water.

"Damned socialism," Klima said.

"What do you mean?"

"It's a bloody pain. They expect us to give concerts free, for nothing. Every day they come up with some new pretext. One day it's for the struggle against imperialism, another time it's the anniversary of the revolution, the next time we're celebrating the birthday of some bigwig. If I want to keep the band together, I've got to go along with everything. You have no idea what they pulled on me today."

"What was that?" she asked listlessly.

"A woman from the local council showed up at rehearsal and started lecturing us on what we're allowed to play and what we're not allowed to play, and in the end she conned us into a free concert for the Youth League. But that's not the worst of it—I'll have to spend all day tomorrow at a stupid conference where they'll go on and on about the role of music in the building of socialism. A whole day shot to hell! And of course they had to pick your birthday!"

"I can't believe they'll keep you there through the evening!"

"No, I guess not. But you can imagine what kind of mood

I'll be in when I come home. That's why I wanted us to enjoy a few pleasant moments tonight," he said, taking his wife by the hand.

"You're sweet," said Mrs. Klima, and Klima realized from her voice that she didn't believe a single word of his story about the next day's conference. She did not dare show this directly, for she knew that her suspicions drove him to fury. But Klima had stopped believing in her apparent trustfulness long ago. Whether he lied or spoke the truth, he always suspected her of suspecting him. There was nothing that could be done about it, he had to go on talking as if he believed that she believed him, and she (with a sad, faraway expression) asked questions about the upcoming conference in order to show him that she did not doubt its authenticity.

Then she went into the kitchen to prepare dinner. She over-salted it. She liked to cook and was extremely good at it (life hadn't spoiled her nor seduced her away from housewifely duties), and Klima knew that the only possible explanation for the poor meal was her unhappiness. In his mind's eye he saw the nervous, abrupt motion of her hand as she poured too much salt into the food, and his heart ached. In each mouthful he seemed to taste her tears and to savor his own guilt. He knew that Kamila was in an agony of jealousy, and that she would not be able to sleep that night; he wanted to kiss her, caress her, comfort her, but he also knew that it would be useless, for her antennae would detect not his tenderness but only his bad conscience.

At last they set out for the movie theater. Klima found a certain reassurance in watching the screen hero, who managed to escape all kinds of treacherous plots with dazzling aplomb. He iden-tified with the self-confident champion, and was buoyed by the feeling that talking Ruzena into an abortion would turn out to be but a trifling challenge, that because of his luck and charm he could not help but triumph easily.

Later they lay down next to each other in the wide bed. He observed her. She was lying on her back, her head pressed into the pillow, her chin slightly lifted and her eyes fixed on the ceiling. In the characteristic tension of her body (she always reminded him of a taut string, and he had once told her that she had the soul of a violin) he suddenly glimpsed the whole essence of her being. Yes, it happened now and again (these were miraculous moments): a single motion or gesture of hers would suddenly reveal to him the entire history of her body and soul. These were moments of a kind of absolute clairvoyance and absolute pathos. This woman who had loved him when he was still a nobody, who was always ready to sacrifice everything for his sake, read his mind and understood all his thoughts so that he could talk to her about Armstrong or Stravinsky, about trifles and serious problems, she was closer to him than anyone else on earth. . . . He imagined this sweet body, this sweet face being no more, and he felt he would not be able to survive her death by a single day. He knew that he was ready to defend her to his last breath, that he was capable of sacrificing his life for her.

But this surge of boundless love was fleeting, for his mind was completely filled with anxiety and fear. He lay next to Kamila. He knew that he loved her immensely. But he was not present in spirit. He stroked her face, but he felt hundreds and hundreds of miles away.

Second Day

1

It was around nine o'clock in the morning when an elegant white car pulled up to the parking lot at the edge of the spa (automobiles were not allowed inside the spa itself).

Down the center of the main avenue ran a strip of lawn with a few trees, sandy walks, and benches painted various colors. The spacious avenue was lined on both sides with buildings. One of them was the Karl Marx House, where nurse Ruzena had her little room. It was in that room that the trumpeter had once spent two fateful hours. Facing the Karl Marx House, on the other side of the avenue, stood the most attractive building in the spa, constructed in turn-of-the-century style, covered with stucco decoration, and boasting a large mosaic over the entrance. This was the only building in the establishment permitted to keep its original name, Richmond House.

"Does Mr. Bartleff still live here?" Klima asked the doorman, and upon receiving an affirmative reply he hurried up the red-carpeted stairs to the second floor. He knocked on the door.

Bartleff came to greet him in his pajamas. Klima, somewhat embarrassed, excused himself for bursting in unannounced, but Bartleff interrupted:

"My dear friend! No need for excuses! I can't imagine a greater pleasure at such an early hour than seeing you again."

He shook Klima's hand and continued: "In this country people don't appreciate mornings. They wake up abruptly, with an alarm clock which breaks up their sleep like the blow of an ax, and they immediately propel themselves into a joyless bustle of activity. Tell me, how can a decent day possibly start in such an unseemly, violent manner! What happens to people who start life each morning with a small shock of alarm from their so aptly named alarm clock? Every day they become a little more conditioned to violence, and a little less accustomed to delight. Believe me, people's characters are decided by their mornings."

Bartleff put his hand on Klima's shoulder and motioned him to an armchair. He continued: "I love those morning hours of inactivity, which are like a beautiful sculpture-lined bridge across which I stroll from night into day, from dream into reality. During those hours, how I long for a miracle! A small miracle, an unexpected encounter which would convince me that my nocturnal dreams do not end with the dawn, and that there is no chasm between adventures of sleep and adventures of the waking day."

The trumpet player watched Bartleff as he paced up and down the room, smoothing his graying hair with his hand, and as he listened to his melodious voice he realized that Bartleff had an ineradicable American accent. His choice of words had a certain charming, old-fashioned quality readily explicable by the fact that he had never lived for any length of time in his ancestral homeland, and that he had learned his mother tongue mainly from his parents.

"And would you believe it, my friend," he added, leaning over Klima with a confiding smile, "nobody in this whole place has been willing to accommodate me. Even the nurses, who are otherwise very obliging, give me dirty looks when I try to inveigle them into spending a cheerful hour with me during breakfast, so that I have to postpone such occasions until evening, when I'm already a bit tired."

He walked over to the phone, which stood on a small table, and asked: "When did you arrive?"

"This morning," said Klima. "I drove up."

"You must be hungry," said Bartleff. He picked up the receiver and ordered two full breakfasts: "Four soft-boiled eggs, cheese, butter, rolls, milk, ham, tea."

In the meantime, Klima studied the room. A large round table, chairs, an armchair, mirror, two couches, a door leading to the bathroom and another door to an adjoining room which—as he recalled—was a small bedroom. Here, in this charming apartment, was where it had all begun. This was where he had been sitting with his drunken fellow musicians when the rich American had held the fateful party for the band and the nurses.

Bartleff said: "That picture opposite you is new since you were here last."

It was only now that the trumpeter noticed the painting, which showed a bearded man with a strange, pale blue disk behind his head, holding a brush and palette. It looked amateurish, but the trumpeter knew that many paintings that seemed awkward were actually the work of famous artists.

"Who painted that?"

"I did," replied Bartleff.

"I didn't know you were an artist," said Klima.

"I like to paint."

"And who is that man?" Klima felt emboldened to ask.

"Saint Lazarus."

"But surely Lazarus was not a painter?"

"This is not the biblical Lazarus, but Saint Lazarus, a monk who lived in the ninth century in Constantinople. He's my patron saint."

"I see," said the trumpeter.

"He was a very strange saint. He was not martyred by pagans because he believed in Christ, but by bad Christians because he loved to paint. As you may be aware, in the eighth and ninth centuries a dour asceticism gained dominance in the Orthodox church, an asceticism hostile to all worldly pleasures. Paintings and statues were in themselves considered sinfully hedonistic. The emperor Theophilus had thousands of beautiful pictures destroyed, and prohibited my beloved Lazarus from painting. But Lazarus knew that painting was his way of praising God and refused to submit. Theophilus had him imprisoned and tortured to force him to give up his brush, but God was merciful and gave Lazarus the strength to bear the most cruel torments."

"That's a beautiful story," said the trumpeter politely.

"It is. But I am sure you had a better reason for coming to see me than to look at my pictures."

At that moment there was a knock on the door and a waiter came in carrying a large tray. He set it on the table and busied himself arranging the breakfast dishes for the two men.

Bartleff asked the trumpeter to sit down at the table and said: "This food will not be so outstanding as to distract us from our conversation. Tell me what's on your mind!"

And so, between mouthfuls, the trumpeter told his story. Now and then, Bartleff interrupted him with probing questions.

2

First of all, Bartleff was puzzled by Klima's coolness toward Ruzena: Why had he ignored all her postcards; why had he pretended not to be there when she phoned; why had he failed to show a single friendly gesture which might have given their one brief night of love a faint, soothing echo?

Klima admitted that he had behaved neither decently nor wisely. But he claimed he could not help it. Any further contact with the girl seemed repellent to him.

This did not satisfy Bartleff. "Any fool can seduce a girl. That's easy. But knowing how to take leave of her—that requires a mature man."

"You're right," the trumpeter admitted sadly, "but my dislike, my insurmountable distaste, is far stronger than all my good intentions."

"Don't tell me you're a misogynist!" exclaimed Bartleff.

"That's what they say about me."

"But you don't seem like the type. You don't look like an impotent or a homosexual!"

"That's true. My problem isn't impotence or homosexuality. It's something much worse," Klima said in a melancholy tone. "I love my own wife. That's my erotic secret, which most people find completely incomprehensible."

This confession was so moving that both men lapsed into silence. After a few moments the trumpeter continued: "Nobody understands this, least of all my wife. She thinks that an unfailing sign of a man's love is his lack of interest in other women. But that's nonsense. Something is always driving me toward some other woman, but as soon as I possess her, a kind of elastic force catapults me back to Kamila. I sometimes have the feeling that I pursue those others only for the sake of the rebound, that wonderful return flight toward my wife (full of tenderness, longing, humility), whom I love more and more with each new act of infidelity."

"So the affair with Ruzena only confirms your steadfast love for your wife."

"Exactly," said the trumpeter. "And a very pleasant confirmation it is, too. Ruzena is quite charming at first sight, and yet her charm completely evaporates within two hours. This has the great advantage that nothing tempts a man to stay longer, and he can look forward to a beautiful takeoff for the return flight home."

"My dear friend, you're a perfect example of the sinfulness of excessive love."

"I thought my love for my wife was just about my only saving grace."

"You were wrong. Your immoderate love for your wife is not a vindication of your heartlessness but its source. Since your wife means everything to you, all other women mean nothing, or, to put it another way, they're mere whores. But this is great blasphemy, great disrespect for God's creatures. My friend, such love is heresy."

3

Bartleff pushed away his empty teacup, rose from the table, and went into the bathroom. Klima heard the sound of running water and then Bartleff's voice: "Do you think people have the right to kill an unborn child?"

Klima had already been somewhat taken aback by the painting of the haloed saint. He remembered Bartleff as a jovial bon vivant, and it never occurred to him that the American might have religious beliefs. Now he was dismayed, for he feared that Bartleff was about to launch into a sermon and that his only oasis in this hostile desert would turn to sand. He said in an uneasy voice: "Are you one of those people who call abortion 'murder'?"

Bartleff kept a lengthy silence. At last he emerged from the bathroom, fully dressed and neatly combed.

" 'Murder' is a word that smells too much of the hangman's noose," he said. "I am concerned about something else. You know, I believe that life is to be accepted totally and completely. That's the very first commandment which has precedence over the other ten. Everything that is about to happen today is in the hands of God, and we know nothing of tomorrow. What I am trying to say is that total acceptance of life means acceptance of the unforeseen. And a child is the essence of the unforeseen, it is the unforeseen itself. You have no idea what the child will grow into, what it will mean for you, and that's why you have to welcome it. Otherwise you're only half alive, you're living like a poor swimmer paddling in the shallows near the shore, while the sea really begins where the water is deep."

The trumpeter objected that the child was not his.

"I don't know how you can be so sure," retorted Bartleff. "For discussion's sake let's assume you're right. But then you must admit in all sincerity that you'd try just as hard to talk Ruzena into an abortion if you knew the baby was yours. You'd do it for the sake of your wife and for the sake of your sinfully excessive conjugal love."

"Yes, I admit it," answered the trumpeter. "I'd urge her to have an abortion under any circumstances."

Bartleff leaned against the frame of the bathroom door and smiled. "I understand you and I am not going to try to change your mind. I am much too old to take on the job of improving the world. I have given you my opinion, and that's that. I will remain your friend even if you disregard my advice, and I will help you even if I don't agree with you."

The trumpet player looked at Bartleff, who delivered the last words in the ringing tones of a kind and wise prophet. There was something majestic about him. It seemed to Klima that everything Bartleff said could serve as homily, a parable, an example, a chapter out of some modern version of the Gospel. He felt like bowing down before him (let's remember that he was under emotional tension, and subject to exaggerated gestures).

"I will do everything in my power to help you," Bartleff repeated. "In a little while we will call on my old friend Dr. Skreta, who will take care of the medical side of the problem. Just tell me how you intend to overcome the objections that Ruzena is bound to raise."

4

That was the third item they discussed. After the trumpeter had elaborated his plan, Bartleff said: "This reminds me of something that happened to me in my wild youth, when I had a job as a dock worker. There was a girl who used to bring us coffee, a girl with an exceptionally kind heart who couldn't say no to anyone. Men usually repay such kindness of heart (and body) by rudeness rather than gratitude. I was the only one who showed her appreciation and courtesy, even though I was the only one who had not gone to bed with her. My gentleness made her fall in love with me, and it would have been a painful insult and humiliation to her if I hadn't slept with her. I did so, but only one single time, and afterward I explained to her that I would always bear a great spiritual love for her, but that further physical intimacy was impossible. She broke into tears and ran óff. When she passed me on the street she'd look the other way, and she gave herself all the more flauntingly to other men. Two months went by, and then she informed me that she was pregnant."

"So your story was just like mine!"

"My friend," said Bartleff, "don't you realize that your story is the experience of all men who ever lived?"

"What did you do?"

"I acted very much the way you're planning to. There is just one difference. You are planning to pretend that you love Ruzena, whereas I really felt genuine love for the girl. To me, she was a pitiful, exploited, and humiliated girl, a poor creature to whom nobody except myself had ever shown any kindness, and she didn't want to lose me. I realized that she could only show it one way, the only way open to her innocent baseness. I couldn't be angry at her for that. Here's what I told her: 'I know perfectly well that it was somebody else who made you pregnant. But I also know that you used this ruse because of your warm feelings for me, and I want to pay back your love with mine. I don't care whose baby it is. If it is your wish, I will marry you.' "

"That was madness!"

"Perhaps. Yet it may well have been more effective than your intended strategy. I kept assuring her that I was extremely fond of her and was serious about marrying her, baby and all. At last the little chippy broke into tears and admitted that she had lied to me. She said that my kindness made her realize that she wasn't worthy of me, and she could never think of marrying me."

The trumpet player lapsed into pensive silence, and Bartleff added: "I wish this story could serve the purpose of a parable for you. Don't try to pretend loving Ruzena. Instead, try to develop genuine fondness for her. Try to feel some sympathy. Even if she's deceiving you, try to see her trick as an instrument of her love. I am sure that she will be unable to resist the power of your kindness, and that she herself will take the necessary steps to avoid hurting you."

Bartleff's words made a great impression on the trumpeter. But as soon as he brought Ruzena more vividly to mind, he realized that the path of love pointed out by Bartleff was too steep for him; it was the path of saints, not of ordinary men.

5

Ruzena was sitting behind a table in the spacious treatment room. Women who had undergone various therapeutic procedures were resting in the beds which lined the walls. She was just checking the treatment cards of two newly arrived patients. She wrote the current date on the two cards, gave the women their locker keys, towels, and long white sheets. Then she looked at her watch and walked to the pool in the rear of the hall (she was wearing only a white coat over her naked body, for the tiled halls were warm and steamy) Some twenty naked women were splashing about in the celebrated healing waters of the pool. She called out the names of three of them, in order to let them know that their assigned period of bathing had come to an end. The ladies obediently scrambled out of the basin, and shaking their pendulous dripping breasts they skipped after Ruzena, who led them to the treatment room up front. There the ladies lay down on vacant beds and Ruzena proceeded to take care of each one in turn: she wrapped each up in a sheet, used a corner of it to wipe the patient's eyes, and finally threw warm blankets over them. They smiled at her, but Ruzena did not smile back.

It is not pleasant to be born in a small town which is invaded every year by ten thousand women and hardly any young men. If a woman plans to live there permanently, by the time she reaches fifteen she is likely to have a perfectly clear picture of all the amorous possibilities life is likely to offer her. As for moving elsewhere—the spa where Ruzena worked was extremely reluctant to release any of its employees, and Ruzena's parents, too, flared up at any hint of a possible move. It was thus understandable that even though Ruzena on the whole fulfilled her duties in a responsible fashion, she was not exactly overflowing with affection toward her patients. Let's cite three reasons for her attitude.

Envy: The women came to the health resort out of the arms of husbands and lovers, out of a glittering world which Ruzena believed to bloom with thousands of opportunities forever beyond her reach, even though she had prettier breasts, longer legs, and more regular features than most of her patients.

In addition to envy, impatience: They came with their colorful histories, while she remained without a history, her destiny unchanging from year to year. It terrified her that she was living out her life in the small town where time was void of events, and although she was still young she was constantly preoccupied with the thought that her life would be over before she had had a chance to start living.

Thirdly, she felt an instinctive distaste for the female multitude which reduced the worth of an individual woman as such. She was surrounded by a depressing glut of breasts, an inflation that made even a bosom as shapely as hers lose value.

With a cross expression she had just finished swaddling the last of the three ladies, when her skinny colleague stuck her head in the room and called out: "Telephone!"

She looked so excited that Ruzena knew at once who was on the phone. She flushed as she picked up the receiver.

Klima greeted her and asked when she would be free.

"I'll be through at three," she answered, "we could get together around four."

Then they discussed the best place to meet. Ruzena suggested the biggest tavern in town, which was open all day. Her skinny colleague, who pressed close and kept her eyes glued on Ruzena's mouth, nodded in agreement. The trumpeter said that he'd rather see Ruzena somewhere else, where they'd be alone, and suggested that they drive into the country with his car.

"What's the point of that? Where would we drive to?" asked Ruzena.

"At least we'd be alone."

"If you're ashamed of me you should have stayed home," said Ruzena. Her friend nodded vigorously.

"I didn't mean it that way," said Klima. "All right then, I'll wait for you at four o'clock in front of the tavern."

"Excellent," said the skinny nurse after Ruzena hung up. "He'd like to meet you in some dark hole-in-the-wall, but you have to make sure that as many people see you as possible."

Ruzena was flustered, and nervous about the meeting. She couldn't remember much about Klima. What did he look like, how did he smile, how did he carry himself? Her one and only encounter with him left only a vague memory. Her colleagues had questioned her eagerly about the famous trumpet player, they wanted to know all about him: what he said, how he looked without clothes, and how he made love. But she was not able to tell them anything definite, and only kept repeating that it was *like a dream.*

This was not a mere cliché. The man with whom she had spent two hours in bed was like a picture on a poster suddenly come to life, taking on three-dimensional substance, warmth, and weight, only to dissolve again into a flat, colorless picture multiplied by thousands of copies and thereby becoming all the more abstract and unreal.

Yes, he had eluded her, his fleeting reality was transformed into an icon that left Ruzena with an uncomfortable sense of his perfection. She could not grasp any concrete detail which would make him descend closer. As long as he remained far away, she had been full of spirited determination, but now that she anticipated his nearness, she felt herself losing courage.

"Good luck!" said the skinny nurse. "I'll keep my fingers crossed!"

6

After Klima had finished his phone conversation with Ruzena, Bartleff took him by the arm and led him to the Marx House, where Dr. Skreta had his office and apartment. Several women were sitting in the waiting room, but without hesitation Bartleff walked up to the door of the examination room and gave four brief knocks. In a few moments a tall, white-coated man came out; his glasses rested on the bridge of an unusually prominent nose. He said, "One moment, please," to the ladies in the waiting room and led the two visitors up the stairs to his second-floor apartment.

"How are you, Maestro?" he greeted the trumpeter after all three had made themselves comfortable. "When are you going to treat us to another concert?"

"Never again, as long as I live," answered Klima. "This place brings me bad luck."

After Bartleff had explained the trumpeter's predicament to the doctor, Klima said: "I would be most grateful for your help. First of all, I'd like to make sure that she's really pregnant. Maybe she's just a little late. Or maybe she's giving me the business. That happened to me once before. It was a blonde that time, too."

"You should stay away from blondes," said Dr. Skreta.

"You are right," agreed Klima. "Blondes are my undoing. Dr. Skreta, you have no idea what a nightmare that was. I kept urging her to have a medical examination. But in the early stages of pregnancy an examination doesn't tell very much. So I wanted them to do a pregnancy test. They inject urine into a mouse—"

"And if the ovaries of the mouse start to bloom, the lady's in trouble," Dr. Skreta interjected.

"She was carrying a sample of morning urine in a small bottle, I went with her, and just as we got to the clinic she dropped the bottle on the sidewalk. I pounced on those slivers as if they were the Holy Grail, trying to save a few precious drops. She did it on purpose, she knew perfectly well that she wasn't pregnant and she only wanted to string out my agony as much as possible."

"Typical blondes' behavior," Dr. Skreta said matter-of-factly.

"You believe that blondes act differently from brunettes?" asked Bartleff, who obviously didn't have much respect for Skreta's knowledge of women.

"Of course," answered Dr. Skreta. "Light and dark—those are the two poles of human character. Dark hair signifies virility, courage, directness, and initiative, whereas fair hair symbolizes femininity, tenderness, and passivity. A blonde is really a woman twice over. That's why a princess has to be fair-haired. And that's why women—to be as feminine as possible—color their hair blond but never black."

"I'd be curious to know how pigments exert an effect on the human soul," said Bartleff.

"It's not a matter of pigments. A blonde, whether real or dyed, unconsciously adapts herself to her hair. She tries to turn herself into a fragile being, a doll, a princess, she demands tenderness and courtesy, gallantry and compliments, she is unable to do anything for herself, all sweetness on the outside and bitchiness on the inside. If dark hair were to become fashionable, the whole world would be a pleasanter place. It would be the most useful social reform ever attempted."

"So you think it likely that Ruzena is just playing with me," said Klima, trying to squeeze some hope out of Skreta's words.

"No. I examined her the day before yesterday. She's pregnant, all right," replied Dr. Skreta.

Bartleff noticed the trumpeter's pallor and said: "Doctor, I believe that you're chairman of the commission that authorizes abortions, aren't you?"

"Yes," said Skreta. "We're meeting this Friday."

"Excellent," said Bartleff. "Something should be done soon, before our friend here collapses altogether. I know that in this country it's a touchy matter to get a legal abortion."

"Extremely touchy," agreed Dr. Skreta. "There are two old hens on the commission who are supposed to represent the voice of the people. They are ugly as sin and hate all the women who come before us. Who are the greatest misogynists in the world? Women! No man—not even Mr. Klima, who's already been twice stuck with a paternity claim—I say, no man feels such resentment against women as women do against their own sex. Why do you think they chase after us men? Only to wound and humiliate their sisters. God put misogyny in the hearts of women because he wanted the human race to multiply."

"I'll forgive you for what you just said, but only because time is pressing and our friend needs help," said Bartleff. "As far as I know, you have the last word on that commission, and those biddies listen to you."

"I do have the last word, that's true," retorted Skreta. "All the same, I've long felt like dropping the whole thing. It's a waste of time, and I don't make a penny on it. Tell me, Maestro, how much do you make on one of your concerts?"

The sum of money mentioned by Klima fascinated the doctor. "I often wonder whether I couldn't earn some easy extra money as a part-time musician. I'm a pretty decent drummer, you know."

"You're a drummer?" Klima asked with as much enthusiasm as he could muster.

"Yes. In our social hall we've got a piano and a set of drums. I give the skins a workout every now and then, when I have a free moment."

"That's fabulous!" exclaimed the trumpeter, glad to have an opportunity to flatter the doctor.

"The trouble is that there's nobody around here to make a passable jazz combo. There's only the pharmacist, who plays fairly decent piano. We've had a couple of good sessions together. Say, I have an idea!" He paused. "When Ruzena has her appointment with the commission . . ."

"I only hope she'll show up!" sighed Klima.

Dr. Skreta waved his arm. "They all show up, don't worry. But the commission requires that the father be present, too, so you will have to come with her. And so you won't have to make the trip just for this nonsense, I suggest you come the day before—that would be this Thursday—and we'll arrange a concert for that evening. Trumpet, piano, drums. *Tres faciunt orkestrum.* With your name on the posters, the hall is bound to be filled to the rafters. What do you say?"

Klima had always guarded the professional quality of his performances with near-fanatical devotion, and only the previous day the doctor's proposal would have seemed preposterous to him. Today, however, he was interested in nothing but the reproductive organs of a certain nurse, and he responded to the doctor's question with polite enthusiasm: "That would be marvelous!"

"Really? You really like the idea?"

"Certainly."

Skreta turned to Bartleff. "And what do you think?"

"I think it's an excellent project. I'm only worried about the timing—two days doesn't give you much in the way of preparation."

By way of reply, Skreta rose and walked over to the phone. He dialed a number but there was no answer. "The number-one order of business is the posters. We've got to start on them right away. But our secretary seems to be out to lunch," he said. "The use of the hall is no problem. The Society for Public Education is sponsoring a lecture on alcoholism on Thursday. A colleague of mine is supposed to speak that night, but he'll be only too happy to cancel on account of illness. Of course, you'll have to get here sometime around noon, to give us time for a little rehearsing. Or do you think that is not necessary?"

"On the contrary," answered Klima, "it's a very good idea. We need to warm up a bit together."

"That's what I thought," said Skreta. "Let's aim for a knock-out repertoire, with a few standbys like 'St. Louis Blues' and 'When the Saints . . .' I've practiced a few solos, too; I'm curious to see how you'll like them. By the way, what are you doing later this afternoon? Maybe we could give it a whirl."

"Unfortunately, this afternoon I'll have to have a session with Ruzena to talk her into an abortion."

Skreta waved his arm. "To hell with that. She'll agree without any fuss."

"All the same, Dr. Skreta," pleaded Klima, "let's leave it for Thursday, if you don't mind."

Bartleff came to Klima's support: "I think Thursday is better, too. Today our friend could hardly be expected to keep his mind on music. Besides, I don't believe he brought his instrument along."

"You're right," admitted Skreta, and proceeded to lead his two visitors to a restaurant across the street. Skreta's nurse caught up with them, however, and in an urgent tone asked the doctor to return to the office. Skreta excused himself and let the nurse take him back to minister to his barren patients.

7

Ruzena had moved into her room in the Karl Marx House about half a year earlier, having previously lived with her parents in a nearby village. During those six months she learned that independence had not brought her the kind of adventure or contentment she had dreamily expected.

Now, returning home from work, she was unpleasantly surprised to find her father ensconced on her living-room couch. This visit came at a bad time as she was anxious to make herself as attractive as possible, to fix her hair and to choose a becoming dress.

"What are you doing here?" she asked irritably. She was angry at the doorman who was chummy with her father and always seemed willing to let him in during her absence.

"We're holding our drill today," said her father. "I have a short break just now."

He was a member of the Citizens' Corps for Civil Order. The medical staff of the spa ridiculed these sixty- and seventy-year-old warriors with their armbands and their pompous fussing, and Ruzena was ashamed of her father's involvement in the outfit.

"I'm surprised you bother with that nonsense," she grumbled.

"You should be proud that your father never loafed a day in his life and never will. We old timers could still teach you youngsters a thing or two."

Ruzena decided to let him talk and to concentrate on her clothes. She opened the wardrobe.

"Yes? Like what?"

"You'd be surprised. Now take this spa: It's known all over the world. It's supposed to be a showplace. And just look at the mess it's in! Children running loose all over the lawns . . ."

"So what?" sighed Ruzena, rummaging through her dresses. None of them appealed to her.

"The brats are bad enough, but those dogs! There's a law on the books that dogs are supposed to be leashed and muzzled. But nobody pays any attention, they all do as they please. Next time take a good look at that park! It's a disgrace!"

Ruzena pulled out a dress and began to change behind the half-open doors of the wardrobe.

"Those mutts piss and shit over everything! Even the sand in the sandbox! Just imagine a baby playing in the sand and dropping a cookie in that mess! No wonder there's so much sickness around. Come here!" Ruzena's father pointed out the window. "Just look! At this very instant I can count four dogs running wild in the park."

Ruzena finished putting on her dress and stepped forward to examine herself in the mirror hanging on the wall. The mirror was small, and she could barely see down to her waist.

"I suppose you're not interested in what I'm saying," said her father.

"Yes, I am," answered Ruzena, backing away from the mirror on tiptoe in order to see the effect the dress was producing on her legs. "Please don't be angry at me, Dad, but I've got to meet somebody in a few minutes and I'm in a hurry."

"As far as I am concerned, the only legitimate dogs are police dogs and hunting dogs," said her father. "But I can't understand why people would want to have a dog in the house. Pretty soon women will stop having children and push baby carriages filled with poodles!"

Ruzena was dissatisfied with the image her mirror reflected. She returned to the wardrobe and started looking for another dress.

"We decided that dogs should be permitted in an apartment house only if the matter is first brought up at a tenants' meeting and none of the tenants objects. We're also recommending raising the fee for dog licenses."

"I wish I had your problems," said Ruzena. It occurred to her how good it was not to have to live at home any longer. Ever since she was a small child her father had gotten on her nerves with his endless sermons and lectures. She longed for a world in which people spoke a different language.

"There's no need for sarcasm. The question of dogs is an important problem. That's not just my opinion, it's the opinion of some of our highest statesmen. I guess they forgot to ask you for your considered opinion. Naturally, you'd tell them the most important thing in the world is choosing the right dress," he added, noticing that his daughter had skipped once more behind the wardrobe for still another change of clothes.

"My dress is a lot more important than your dogs, that's for sure," she snapped, once more stretching in front of the mirror. She did not like herself any better this time. But dissatisfaction with her own looks was slowly changing into defiance; the thought that the trumpeter was going to see her in a cheap and unattractive dress, whether he liked it or not, gave her a certain spiteful satisfaction.

"It's a matter of hygiene," continued her father. "Our towns will never get any cleaner as long as the sidewalks are full of dog shit. And it's a question of morality, too. It just isn't right for people to cluck and coo over a bunch of stupid mutts."

Something was happening which Ruzena did not realize: her defiance was imperceptibly, mysteriously merging with her father's indignation. She no longer felt such strong distaste for him; on the contrary, she was unconsciously using his angry words as a source of energy.

"We never had a dog in the house, and nobody missed it," he said.

She continued to gaze into the mirror and felt that with her pregnancy a new sense of power had grown inside her. What if she didn't like her own looks? The fact remained that the trumpeter had driven up to see her and had humbly asked her to meet him. In fact (she glanced at her watch) he was probably waiting for her at this very moment.

"We'll put things in order, just wait and see!" laughed her father, and she answered gently, almost with a smile:

"I hope so, Dad. But now I really must be off."

They went downstairs together and said goodbye in front of the entrance to the Karl Marx House. Ruzena walked slowly toward the tavern.

8

Klima had never succeeded in identifying completely with the role of a famous popular artist. In the midst of his current private worries, his public fame seemed particularly bothersome. As soon as he entered the tavern and saw his blown-up image staring down from a poster left over from the last concert, a sense of gloomy anxiety seized him. He led Ruzena into the dining room, uneasily glancing around for signs of recognition among the guests. He was afraid of their eyes, it seemed to him that he was being scrutinized, that his facial expression and gestures were no longer under his own control. He felt himself a target of several inquisitive looks. He tried to ignore them and aimed for a table at the back, where there was a large window with a view of the park.

As soon as they were seated he smiled at Ruzena, stroked her arm, and said that her dress became her. She demurred modestly, and he gallantly insisted and tried to prolong the conversation on the subject of her charms. He told her that he was amazed by her appearance. He had been thinking of her throughout the past two months, and his imagination had painted a picture of her which fell far short of the reality. And he said that even though he had thought about her in a warm and loving way, she was even lovelier in person than in his imagination.

Ruzena countered that the trumpeter had totally ignored her for two months, which was rather peculiar, considering that he claimed to have thought about her so much.

He had prepared himself thoroughly for this objection. He heaved a deep sigh and told the girl that she could have no possible idea of the agony he had been going through during those two months. She asked him to explain, but he said he preferred not to go into the sordid details. He only said that he had been the victim of terrible ingratitude, and that he had suddenly found himself all alone in the world, without a single friend.

He was worried that Ruzena might press him for further details about his travails and that he might easily become entangled in his own lies. But his concern proved needless. Ruzena listened eagerly and was pleased to have found an explanation for Klima's two-month silence, but she was indifferent to the exact nature of his misfortunes. The only thing that interested her about his melancholy months was their melancholy.

"I thought a lot about you and I would have liked to help you," she said.

"I was so disgusted with the whole world that I didn't want

to see a soul. Gloomy people don't make good company."

"I was lonely and sad, too."

He stroked her hand. "I know."

"I've known for a long time that we are having a baby together. And you never called me. I would have had the baby anyway, regardless, even if you had not come, even if you never wanted to see me again. I told myself that even if I were left all alone, at least I'd have your baby. I'd never get rid of it. Never . . ."

Klima was terror-stricken.

Fortunately, the waiter, who had been lazily shuffling among the tables, now made his appearance and asked for their order.

"A brandy," said the trumpeter softly, then quickly corrected himself: "Make that two brandies."

More silence.

Ruzena whispered: "I wouldn't let them take my baby from me. Not for anything in the world."

He recovered his senses at last. "Don't say that. After all, you're not the only one involved. A child is not just a woman's problem. It concerns both people. And both of them have to work things out together, or else they are in serious trouble."

As soon as the words were out of his mouth he realized that he had just indirectly admitted that he was the father of the child, and that all subsequent conversation with Ruzena would have to be based on that assumption. He was acting according to plan, this was a concession thoroughly weighed in advance; all the same, Klima was frightened by the sound of his own words.

The waiter came back with two brandies. "You are Mr. Klima the trumpet player," he said.

"Yes."

"The girls in the kitchen recognized you. That's you on the poster!"

"Yes."

"I hear you're the idol of all the girls from twelve to seventy," said the waiter, and turned to Ruzena: "The women will all be dying with envy. Don't let them scratch your eyes out!" As he was going back to the kitchen he turned around several times, smiling with insolent familiarity.

Ruzena repeated: "I could never let them take the baby away. And someday you'll be happy, too, to have the child. I don't want anything from you. Don't think for a moment that I am going to bother you. You don't have a thing to worry about. This is my problem, and if you like you can leave it completely up to me."

Nothing makes a man more nervous than this kind of reassurance. Klima felt his strength rapidly ebbing; he despaired of salvaging anything at all and lapsed into silence. Ruzena's last words echoed through this silence as if to mock his utter helplessness.

But then he thought of his wife and realized that he must not surrender. He slid his hand across the marble tabletop until it was touching Ruzena's. He squeezed her fingers and said: "Let's forget the baby for a moment. The baby is not the main thing, anyway. You think the two of us have nothing else to talk about? You think I drove out here to see you for the sake of a fetus?"

Ruzena shrugged.

"You've no idea how much I missed you. It's funny, we've only known each other such a short time, and yet there wasn't a single day that I didn't think about you."

He paused. Ruzena said: "Not one word from you for two whole months! And I wrote you twice!"

"Don't be angry with me, darling," said the trumpeter. "I didn't answer you on purpose. I was afraid of the stormy feelings inside me. I resisted falling in love. I wanted to write you a long letter, I actually covered sheets and sheets of paper, but then I threw them all away. I have never been so much in love before, and it terrified me. And then there was something else. Why shouldn't I admit it? I wanted to make sure that my feelings were the real thing, that it wasn't just a magic spell that would vanish as quickly as it had come. I told myself: If at the end of one month I am still this deeply in love, then I'll know it's the real thing and not an illusion."

Ruzena said softly: "And what do you think now? Was it only an illusion?"

As soon as Ruzena said this, the trumpeter sensed that his plan was beginning to work. He therefore continued to hold the girl's hand and talked on and on, with greater and greater ease. He said that at this moment, sitting here and looking at her, he realized that there was no need to subject his feelings to any further tests, because everything had become quite clear in his mind. There was no point in talking about the baby, for it was Ruzena who was important to him, and not her baby. That unborn child had merely called him to Ruzena's side; that was its real significance. Yes, the baby inside her had brought him here to the spa and shown him how much he loved Ruzena, and for this reason (he raised his glass of brandy) he was now drinking to the baby's health.

At once, he became terrified by the fateful toast to which his verbal enthusiasm had led him. But it was too late, the words were out of his mouth. Ruzena lifted her glass, whispered, "Yes—to our child!" and took a sip of brandy.

The trumpeter tried to bury the unfortunate toast in a flood of words and proclaimed anew that he had thought of Ruzena every single hour of every day.

She said she was sure that in the big city he was pursued by flocks of fascinating and beautiful women.

He countered that he was fed up with their arrogance and artifice. They put on airs but Ruzena was a true queen, and he felt it was a terrible pity that he was condemned to be so far away from her. Couldn't she move to the capital?

She said she would love to do that, but it was not easy to find a job in the city.

He smiled indulgently and said he knew many influential people, and it would not be difficult to place her in some clinic or hospital.

He went on talking in this manner for a long time, continuing to hold her hand, so he failed to notice that a young girl had approached their table. Not caring that she was disturbing them, she burst out brashly: "You are Mr. Klima! I recognized you at once! Could I have your autograph?"

Klima blushed. He became aware that he had just been squeezing Ruzena's hand and making a declaration of love to her in a public place before the eyes of everybody present. He felt as if he were sitting on the stage of an amphitheater with the whole world turned into an amused public watching with gleeful spite his desperate existential struggle.

The girl handed him a piece of paper. Klima longed to get the autographing over with as quickly as possible, but neither he nor the girl had anything to write with.

"Have you got a pen?" he whispered to Ruzena.

Ruzena shook her head and the girl went back to her table. Now her whole group of companions took advantage of the opportunity to meet a famous musician. They clustered around Klima, handed him a ballpoint, and kept tearing pieces of paper out of a notebook for Klima to sign.

In terms of the prearranged plan of action, this was fine: the greater the number of people who witnessed their intimacy, the greater confidence Ruzena would have that her love affair with Klima was still going strong. But in Klima's state of mind such rational thoughts were engulfed by a turmoil of anxiety, and he was on the verge of panic. He became obsessed with the idea that Ruzena was in league with all those people, and that they all would bear witness against him in a paternity suit: "Yes, we saw them, they were huddling together like a pair of lovers, he was stroking her hand and gazing rapturously into her eyes. . . ."

These anxieties were aggravated by the trumpeter's vanity; he did not consider Ruzena sufficiently attractive to merit his public show of affection. In that respect he was somewhat unfair. She was actually much prettier than he thought at that moment. Just as love makes the beloved woman more beautiful, the anxiety produced by a feared woman makes all her imperfections grow to disproportionate size. . . .

At last they were left alone and Klima said: "I don't like this place at all. Wouldn't you like to go for a drive?"

She was curious about his car and agreed. Klima paid the bill and they went out. Opposite the restaurant was a small park with a yellow sand promenade. Some ten men were lined up in a row along the promenade. Most of them were of advanced age. On the sleeves of their wrinkled jackets they sported red armbands, and each was holding a long pole.

Klima was horrified. "What in the world is that?"

Ruzena said quickly: "It's nothing. Come on, show me your car," and tried to pull him away.

Klima, however, could not take his eyes off the oldsters. He simply could not grasp the purpose of the long poles equipped with wire loops at one end. The men might have been old-fashioned lamplighters, or hunters of flying fish, or home guardsmen armed with a secret weapon.

As he was watching, it seemed to him that one of them was smiling at him. That scared him. He was afraid that he was beginning to suffer from hallucinations and to imagine that people were spying on him. He let Ruzena lead him away briskly to the parking lot.

9

"I'd love to take you somewhere far away," he said. He had one hand on the steering wheel, the other arm was around Ruzena's shoulders. "South. I'd love to drive with you down long highways by the sea. Do you know Italy?"

"No."

"Promise me you'll come with me."

"Aren't you overdoing it a bit?"

Ruzena said it out of a sense of modesty, but the trumpeter was alarmed lest the girl's "overdoing it" referred to his whole demagogic speech.

"Yes, I am overdoing it. My ideas are always extravagant. That's how I am. But, unlike other people, I try to make my extravagant ideas come true. Believe me, there is nothing more beautiful in the world than a grand dream that's been turned into reality. I wish my life were just one single extravagant dream. I wish we'd never have to return to the spa, I wish we could just drive on and on until we reached the sea. I'd find a job in some band and we'd roam from one seaside town to the next."

He stopped the car at a scenic spot. They stepped out. He suggested a walk in the woods. For a while they walked along a path and then sat down on a wooden bench left over from the era when people did not use cars so much and outings in the country were more popular. He kept his arm around her, and suddenly said in a sad voice:

"You know, everybody thinks that my life is a ball. Nothing could be further from the truth. In reality I have been very unhappy. Not for just the last few months, but for a long, long time."

The trumpeter's words about a trip to Italy had seemed unrealistic to her (she knew that permission to travel abroad freely was extremely difficult to obtain) and evoked in her a vague distrust. In contrast, the mournfulness which now wafted from his words smelled sweet to her. She savored it like the aroma of well-roasted pork.

"How could you, of all people, be unhappy?"

"I can, believe me," sighed the trumpet player.

"You're famous, you have a fancy car, money, a beautiful wife. . . ."

"Beautiful she may be . . ." the trumpeter said bitterly.

"I know," said Ruzena. "She's no longer young. She's as old as you, isn't she?"

The trumpeter realized that Ruzena had succeeded in get-

ting personal information about his wife, and this made him angry.
He controlled himself, however: "Yes, we're the same age."

"Oh well, you've got no problems on that score. You're not
really old. You look almost boyish."

"But a man needs a woman younger than he is," said Klíma.
"Especially an artist. I need youth, Ruzena, you have no idea how
I love your youth. Sometimes I think I can't stand it any longer, I
have such a desire to free myself, to start all over. Ruzena, that phone
call yesterday—it made chills run up and down my spine. I had the
feeling that it was a call from fate itself."

"Is that the truth?" she asked softly.

"Why do you think I called you right back? I had a strong
feeling that I mustn't delay, that I must see you right away, at once,
at once. . . ." He paused and gazed into her eyes. "Do you love me?"

"Yes. And you?"

"I love you very much," he said.

"Me, too."

He leaned over and kissed her on the mouth. It was a clean
mouth, a youthful mouth, a pretty mouth with curved soft lips and
well-brushed teeth, everything about it was pleasant; after all, two
months ago he had found this mouth extremely kissable. But precisely because he had found it so alluring, he perceived it through
a fog of desire and knew nothing of its real likeness: the tongue
appeared to him like a flame, the saliva like an intoxicating potion.
Only a mouth that had no attraction for him was a *real* mouth, a
busy opening through which passed loads of dumplings, potatoes,
and soups, a mouth with cavity-pocked teeth and saliva that was not
an elixir but the twin of a glob of spit. The tongue that was now
filling the trumpeter's mouth was a real tongue, a distasteful morsel
that he could neither swallow nor spit out.

The kiss was over at last. They walked on. Ruzena was almost
happy, and yet she was aware that the problem which had caused
her to telephone the trumpeter, the problem which had brought him
here, was being oddly bypassed in their conversation. She had no
desire to discuss it at length. On the contrary, the present subject

of their talk seemed far more pleasant and important. Nevertheless, she wanted the neglected problem to be acknowledged, even if only discreetly, unobtrusively, modestly. Thus, when Klima assured Ruzena—after various declarations of love—that he would do everything in his power to make a new life for her, she remarked:

"That's very good of you, but you have to remember that I am no longer just one person."

"Yes," said Klima. He knew that this was the moment he had feared all along; the most vulnerable point in his whole demagogic stratagem.

"Yes, you're right," he repeated. "You are no longer alone, but that's not what counts. I want to be with you because I love you, and not because you're pregnant."

"Yes," sighed Ruzena.

"Nothing is more awful than two people getting married for no other reason than that they slipped up and produced a baby. As a matter of fact, darling, to tell the truth—I want you to be the same as before! There should be just the two of us, with nobody else coming between. Do you understand me?"

"Oh no, that's impossible! I can't do that! I'd never do a thing like that," protested Ruzena.

She said it vehemently, but her resistance did not spring from any fundamental conviction. After all, it was only two days earlier that her pregnancy had been confirmed and this certainty was still too fresh in her mind to have given rise to any new plan or course of action. She was, however, conscious of her pregnancy as a great event in her life and as an opportunity that would not soon come again. She felt like a pawn in a game of chess which, having reached the end of the chessboard, has turned into a queen. She savored her unexpected new power. She saw that her call had set into motion all sorts of events: the famous trumpeter left his home to rush to her side, to escort her around in his beautiful car, to make love to her. Clearly, there was a connection between her pregnancy and this sudden power, and giving up the one might mean forfeiting the other.

Thus the trumpeter had to keep on rolling his boulder. "Darling, I am not longing for a family. I am longing for love. You are my love, and a baby turns every love into a family. Into boredom. Worries. Chores. A beloved woman becomes an ordinary mother. I can't see you as a mother. You are my beloved, and I don't want to share you with anyone. Not even with a baby."

These were gallant words, Ruzena was happy to hear them, but she shook her head all the same. "No, I couldn't do that. It's your baby! How could I get rid of your baby?"

He could think of no new argument, so he kept on repeating the same words, worried that she might see through their insincerity.

"You're past thirty already," she said. "Haven't you ever wished you had a child?"

Actually, the truth was that he hadn't. He loved Kamila so much that a child would have seemed in the way. When he had expressed this idea to Ruzena a few moments back, it was not pure fiction. He had been saying the same thing to his wife for many years, sincerely and honestly.

"You've been married for six years and have no children. I was so happy to be able to give you a baby."

He realized that everything was turning against him. The abundance of his love for Kamila appeared to Ruzena as Kamila's lack of fertility and encouraged her to impudent presumption.

It was getting cooler, the sun was nearing the horizon, time was fleeing, and he kept on repeating what he had already told her, while she kept shaking her head, *no, no, I couldn't*. He felt he was in a blind alley, he didn't know which way to turn and everything seemed on the edge of disaster. He was so nervous that he forgot to hold her hand, to kiss her, or to speak in a tender tone of voice. With a start he realized this and tried to rouse himself. He came to a halt, smiled at her, and embraced her. It was the embrace of fatigue. He pressed her close, his cheek touching hers; actually, he was leaning on her, resting, panting, because the road ahead appeared too steep for his waning strength.

But Ruzena too was at the end of her wits. She could think

of no further arguments either, and she knew that stubborn negation was hardly the way to win a man's heart.

The embrace lasted a long time, and after Klima released her from his arms she bowed her head and said in a resigned tone: "All right, then tell me what to do."

Klima did not dare trust his ears. It came so suddenly and unexpectedly, and it was an enormous relief, so enormous that he had to control himself not to reveal it. He stroked the girl's face and said that Dr. Skreta was a good friend of his, and all she had to do was show up in three days at a hearing. They'd go there together. There was nothing to be afraid of.

Ruzena did not protest, and he gathered new determination to finish the battle. He put his arm around her shoulder, drew her close again, and again kissed her (his joy was so great that Ruzena's lips were once more veiled by a mist). He kept repeating his wish that Ruzena move to the capital. He even repeated his speech about a trip to the south.

By then the sun had already sunk below the horizon, the woods were turning dark, and the moon was rising over the treetops. They walked back to the car. As they reached the highway they suddenly found themselves in the glare of a sharp beam of light. At first they thought it came from the headlights of a passing car, but then it became apparent that the light was following them. It came from a motorcycle parked on the other side of the road. A man was sitting on it, watching them intently.

"Come on, let's go quickly," said Ruzena.

As they drew near to the car the man got off his vehicle and walked toward them. The trumpeter saw only a dark silhouette outlined by the motorcycle headlight.

"Wait!" The man rushed at Ruzena. "I have to talk to you! Listen to me! I've got to see you!" he shouted excitedly.

The trumpeter, too, was nervous and bewildered and could no longer feel anything but a vague irritation at the stranger's lack of manners.

"The young lady is with me," he said sharply.

"I've got a few words to say to you, too!" the man yelled at the trumpeter. "You think just because you're famous you can get away with anything you like! You think you can lead girls around by the nose! It's all very easy when you're a big-shot celebrity!"

As the motorcyclist momentarily turned his attention to Klima, Ruzena quickly took advantage of the situation and scrambled into the car. She rolled up the window and turned on the radio. Loud music blared through the car. The trumpeter, too, climbed in and slammed the door shut. Through the windshield they saw the outline of the shouting man and his gesticulating arms.

"He's always chasing me. He's a maniac," said Ruzena. "Let's get out of here!"

10

He parked the car, escorted Ruzena to the Karl Marx House, gave her a parting kiss. As she disappeared into the doorway he felt as tired as if he had just spent a dozen sleepless nights. It was late in the evening, he was hungry, and he felt he didn't even have the strength to sit down behind the wheel and drive. He longed for some comforting words from Bartleff, and set out across the park to Richmond House.

As he reached the entrance, he noticed a large poster lit up by the light of a streetlamp. His name was written across the top in large, awkward letters, with the names of Skreta and the pharmacist appearing in smaller letters below. The poster had been done by hand, and featured an amateurish drawing of a golden trumpet.

The promptness with which Dr. Skreta had organized the promotion of the concert seemed like a good omen; the doctor was apparently a man who could be depended on.

Klima climbed the stairs and knocked on Bartleff's door.

There was no answer.

He knocked once more. Still no answer.

Before he had time to consider whether he was being indiscreet (the American was known for his numerous affairs with women), his hand had already pushed down the door handle. The door was not locked. The trumpeter entered, then stopped short, startled. The room was quite dark except for a glow emanating from one corner. The glow did not resemble the white light of a fluorescent tube nor the yellowish light of an electric bulb. It was blue, a strange blue aura.

By the time the trumpeter's sluggish mind had caught up with his rash hand, it occurred to him that he was being rude in entering someone else's room without invitation, and at a late hour to boot. Ashamed of his lack of manners, he stepped back into the hall and quickly closed the door behind him. He was bewildered, however, and did not leave but remained standing at the door, trying to grasp the mysterious phenomenon he had just seen. It occurred to him that the American might have been tanning himself under an ultraviolet lamp. But suddenly the door opened and Bartleff appeared. He was fully dressed, and wearing the same clothes he had had on in the morning. He smiled at the trumpeter. "I'm glad you stopped by. Come in."

The trumpeter entered with curiosity, but found that the room was lit by an ordinary fixture hanging from the ceiling.

"I'm afraid I am disturbing you," said the trumpeter.

"Not at all," answered Bartleff, pointing toward the window; it was from that direction that the light seen by the trumpeter a while ago had seemed to emanate. "I was sitting there, thinking. That's all."

"When I stepped in a moment ago—excuse me for having barged in like that—I saw a strange kind of glow."

"A glow?" Bartleff laughed. "You mustn't take that pregnancy so hard. It's giving you hallucinations."

"Maybe my eyes didn't have time to adjust. It was very dark in the hall."

"Maybe," said Bartleff. "But tell me about your meeting with Ruzena!"

The trumpeter recounted the story, and after a while Bartleff interrupted: "You must be hungry!"

The trumpet player nodded. Bartleff opened the cupboard and pulled out a package of crackers and a can of ham, which he immediately proceeded to open.

Klima continued to talk, eagerly gulping down his supper and looking inquisitively at Bartleff.

"I think everything will turn out all right," Bartleff reassured him.

"And what do you think of the man on the motorcycle?"

Bartleff shrugged. "I don't know. But in any case, it doesn't matter anymore."

"That's true. My problem right now is how to explain to Kamila why the conference is taking so long."

It was already quite late. Refreshed and soothed, the trumpeter climbed into his car and set off for the capital. A big round moon lighted his way.

Third Day

1

It was Wednesday morning and the spa once more awoke to its round of busy activity. Jets of water began streaming into tubs, masseurs flexed their arms, fresh linen was being readied, and a private car had just pulled into the parking lot. Not the luxurious roadster that had occupied the same spot the day before, but a plain, ordinary-looking sedan. A man of about forty-five was behind the wheel, and he was alone. The back seat was piled high with several suitcases.

The man got out, locked the car, handed some change to the attendant, and walked toward the Karl Marx House. He wound his way through the hall until he came to Dr. Skreta's office. After crossing the waiting room, he knocked on the examining-room door. A nurse stuck her head out, the man introduced himself, and in a few moments Dr. Skreta appeared:

"Jakub! When did you get here?"

"This minute."

"That's great! We've got so much to go over. . . . Listen," he said after a moment's thought. "I can't leave now. Come with me. I'll lend you a coat."

Jakub was not a physician, and he had never seen the inside of a gynecologist's office. But Dr. Skreta had already grasped him by the arm and led him into a white-walled room, where a disrobed woman was lying on her back with her legs spread wide apart.

"Give the doctor a coat," Skreta said to his nurse, who opened a cabinet and handed a crisply starched white coat to Jakub. "Come over here." Skreta turned to Jakub. "I want you to confirm my diagnosis." The woman seemed quite pleased to have another expert explore the mysteries of her ovaries, which in spite of all efforts had thus far failed to bring forth a descendant.

Dr. Skreta resumed his examination of the patient's private

parts, uttered a few Latin expressions to which Jakub mumbled approval, and then asked: "How long will you stay here?"

"A day."

"Just one day? That's too bad, that will give us hardly any time to talk."

"It hurts when you touch me like that," said the woman with the raised legs.

"It always hurts a bit, that's quite normal," said Jakub to amuse his friend.

"Yes, the doctor is right," said Skreta, "that's nothing. Quite normal. I will prescribe a series of injections for you. I want you to come here every day, first thing in the morning, and the nurse will give you your injection. You can get dressed now."

"I really came to say goodbye to you," said Jakub.

"What do you mean?"

"I am going abroad. They finally gave me permission to emigrate."

The woman patient finished dressing and took leave of Skreta and his colleague.

"That's quite a surprise! I had no idea!" exclaimed Dr. Skreta. "I'll send these women away so that we'll have a little time together."

"But, Doctor," interjected the nurse, "you did the same thing yesterday. By the end of the week we'll be way behind schedule!"

"All right, send in the next one," sighed Skreta.

The nurse called in the next patient. The two men glanced at her absentmindedly, noting that she was prettier than the previous one. Dr. Skreta asked her whether the baths were making her feel better, and then requested her to disrobe.

"It took an awfully long time before they gave me my passport. Once I got it in my hands, I was ready to leave in two days. I didn't even bother to say goodbye to anyone."

"That makes me feel all the happier that you stopped by here," said Skreta. He asked the young woman to climb up on the examining table. He put on a rubber glove and inserted his hand into her vagina.

"I wanted to see nobody except you and Olga," said Jakub. "I hope she's all right."

"She's fine," said Skreta, but it was obvious from his voice that he was answering mechanically. His total concentration was on the patient. "We'll have to perform a little operation," he said. "Don't worry, it won't hurt a bit." He walked over to the glass-enclosed cabinet and pulled out a syringe. In place of a needle it had a short plastic nozzle.

"What's that?" asked Jakub.

"After all these years I have hit on a new approach which is highly effective. You may think it selfish of me, but for the time being I prefer to keep it my secret."

"Am I really all right?" asked the woman with the raised legs, in a tone that was more coy than fearful.

"Absolutely," answered Dr. Skreta, dipping the tip of the syringe into a test tube which he was holding with great care. Then he stepped closer to the patient, inserted the syringe between her legs, and squeezed the plunger.

"That didn't hurt, did it?"

"No," she answered.

"The other reason I came was to give you back your pill," said Jakub.

Once again, Dr. Skreta barely grasped Jakub's meaning. His attention was fully taken up by his patient. He scrutinized her from head to toe with a serious, pensive face and said: "In your case it would really be a pity not to have children. You have nice long legs, a well-structured pelvis, a solid rib cage, and very pleasant features."

He chucked her under the chin and added: "A nice firm jaw bone, too. Everything is well modeled."

Then he grasped her thigh. "And you have wonderfully firm bones. They practically shine from beneath your muscles."

He continued to savor his patient's well-proportioned figure and to feel her body. She neither protested nor giggled coquettishly, for the seriousness of the doctor's interest lifted his gestures above any possible suggestion of immorality.

At last he motioned for her to get dressed, and turned to his friend: "Sorry, what were you saying?"

"That I came to return your pill to you."

"What pill?"

While getting dressed the patient said: "You think there's hope for me, Doctor?"

"I am very satisfied," answered Dr. Skreta. "Everything is coming along just fine, and both of us—you and I—can look forward to success."

The woman thanked the doctor and left. Jakub said: "You once obtained a certain pharmaceutical preparation for me which nobody else was willing to give me. Now that I am leaving the country, I don't think that I'll have any more need for it and I ought to give it back to you."

"That's all right, you can keep it. A pill like that might come in handy anywhere."

"No, no. The pill is really the property of this country. I don't want to take anything with me that does not belong to me."

"Can I call in the next patient?" the nurse asked.

"Send all those females home," said Dr. Skreta. "I did my share of work today. That last patient who just walked out is sure to have a baby, I'd bet on it. That's enough for a day's work, isn't it?"

The nurse gave Dr. Skreta a look which was affectionate yet firm. The doctor understood: "All right, all right. Don't send them away, just tell them I'll be back in half an hour."

"That's what you said yesterday, too, and then I had to go out and nab you in the street."

"Don't worry, I'll be back in thirty minutes flat," said Skreta. He hung his friend's overcoat on the rack, then led him out the door and across the park toward Richmond House.

2

They climbed the stairs to the second floor and walked down a long red carpet to the end of the hall. Dr. Skreta opened a door and entered a small but pleasant room.

"It's wonderful the way you always manage to put me up somewhere."

"They've set a couple of rooms aside for me at the end of this hall for my bigwig patients. Right next to you there is a beautiful corner apartment which was used in the old days by industrialists and cabinet ministers. I've put one of my prize patients there, a rich American whose family comes from this part of the world. We've become good friends."

"And where does Olga live?"

"In the Marx House, like me. It's not a bad place, don't worry."

"I'm certainly glad you took her under your wing. How is she doing?"

"She has the usual problems of high-strung women."

"It's no wonder. I wrote you what she had gone through in her life."

"Most women come to this place to become fertile. But your ward would be better off without much fertility. Have you ever seen her naked?"

"Good Lord, no!" exclaimed Jakub.

"Then take a good look at her sometime. Her breasts are tiny and hang from her chest like a pair of prunes. You can count her ribs. From now on you should pay more attention to rib cages. A proper rib cage should be aggressive, outward-going, expansive as if it wanted to encompass as much space as possible. Some rib cages, though, are on the defensive, they retreat from the world. They are like straitjackets which get tighter and tighter until they choke a person to death. That's what her rib cage is like. Ask her to show it to you."

"I'll do nothing of the kind."

"You're afraid that if you ever saw her bosom you'd no longer want her as your ward."

"On the contrary," said Jakub, "I'm afraid I'd feel still sorrier for her."

"By the way," said Skreta, "that American is a very interesting character."

Jakub asked: "Where can I find her?"

"Whom?"

"Olga."

"You won't be able to catch her now. She's having her treatments. She's supposed to spend the whole morning in the pool."

"I'd hate to miss her. Is there no way to call up the pool?"

Dr. Skreta lifted the receiver and dialed a number without interrupting his conversation with Jakub: "I'll introduce you to him and I want you to analyze him for me. You're an excellent psychologist. He and I have some plans. . . ."

"What kind of plans?" asked Jakub, but Skreta was already speaking into the receiver:

"Is this nurse Ruzena? How are you? . . . Don't worry about that, in your condition that's quite normal. Listen, I called up to find out whether my patient is there, you know, the one who lives right next door to you. . . . She's there? Then tell her someone is here to see her. . . . Yes, that's fine, he'll be waiting for her in front of the pool at twelve o'clock."

Skreta hung up. "You heard that. She'll meet you at noon. Damn it, what were we talking about just now?"

"About the American."

"Oh yes," said Skreta. "He's a fascinating fellow. I cured his wife. She was sterile."

"And what's his problem?"

"Cardiac trouble."

"You said that you and he had some plans?"

"It's really a rotten shame," said Skreta angrily, "what a doctor in this country has to go through to be able to live on a decent level! Tomorrow the famous trumpeter Klima is coming. And I have to accompany him on the drums, just to make a little pocket money."

Jakub thought that Skreta was joking, but he pretended to take his friend's remark seriously: "What do you mean? You play the drums?"

"You bet. What choice have I got, now that I'm about to have a family?"

"What?" This time Jakub was genuinely surprised. "Family? Don't tell me you got married!"

"I have."

"To Kveta?"

Kveta was a physician at the spa. She and Skreta had been intimate friends for years, but he had always managed to elude marriage.

"Yes, to Kveta," said Skreta. "You remember how on Sundays she and I would always stroll up to the observatory?"

"So you got married at last," said Jakub mournfully.

"Each time we climbed up the observatory tower, Kveta tried to talk me into getting married," continued Skreta. "And I was always so knocked out and winded by the time I reached the top that I felt old and tired and ready for the married state. But I always managed to control myself in the nick of time; on the way down all my zip and energy would come back to me and I would be perfectly content to stay single. One fateful Sunday, though, Kveta took me up by a roundabout way and the climb was so hard that I gasped 'yes' even before we reached the top. Now we're expecting a baby and I have to think about money. The American paints religious pictures. They could bring in quite a bundle. What do you think?"

"You believe there's a market here for religious pictures?"

"Of course! Whenever there's a pilgrimage we could set up

a stall right next to the church and we'd sell hundreds of them! We'd both be rich! I could be his agent and split the profits with him."

"What does he say?"

"That bastard has so much money he doesn't know what to do with it. I can't seem to talk him into any kind of business deal," said Dr. Skreta, and cursed under his breath.

3

Olga saw perfectly well that nurse Ruzena was waving at her from the edge of the pool, but she kept on swimming and pretended not to notice.

The two women did not like each other. Dr. Skreta had put Olga in a room next to Ruzena's. Ruzena was in the habit of playing the radio loud, and Olga liked quiet. She pounded on the wall on several occasions, to which the nurse responded by turning up the radio even louder.

Now Ruzena was patiently waving her arms, until at last she succeeded in getting the patient's attention and telling her that she had a visitor from the capital and that he would meet her at twelve.

Olga guessed at once that it was Jakub and she was filled with enormous pleasure. This pleasure surprised her; she asked herself why she was so happy to hear that he was coming. Olga was one of those modern women who like to divide themselves into a being that experiences and a being that observes.

But now even Olga the Observer was enjoying herself. She was very well aware that it was quite improper for the other, experiencing Olga to be so happy, and because Olga the Observer was spiteful this impropriety gave her pleasure. She amused herself trying to imagine how frightened Jakub would be if he knew of the intensity of her joy.

The hands on the clock over the pool showed a quarter to twelve. Olga tried to picture Jakub's face if she were to throw herself around his neck and kiss him passionately. She swam to the edge of the pool, climbed out, and went to the cabin to change. It annoyed her that she hadn't learned of his visit sooner. She would have put on a more attractive outfit. Now she was wearing a gray, uninteresting dress which spoiled her mood.

At times, such as back in the swimming pool, she was completely oblivious to her looks. But now she was standing in front of a small mirror and saw herself in her dull gray dress. Only a few minutes ago she was maliciously smiling at the thought of hugging and kissing Jakub. But that occurred to her in the pool, while she was floating like a disembodied, free spirit. Now, once more enclosed in a body and a dress, she felt far removed from that buoyant self. She knew that she had reverted to the Olga whom Jakub unfortunately always saw: a pitiful girl in need of help.

If Olga had been just a bit less brainy perhaps she might have considered herself quite pretty. But since she was intelligent, she saw herself as far more unattractive than she actually was. In reality, she was neither pretty nor homely, and any man with average criteria of beauty would have gladly spent the night with her.

Olga the Observer chided her flesh-and-blood sister: What difference did it make how she looked? Why torment herself, anxiously peering into the mirror? Was she nothing but an object for male eyes? Why not make herself independent of surface appearance? Didn't women have the same right to such freedom as men?

She stepped out of the building and saw his face as it broadened into a good-natured smile. She knew that instead of shaking her hand he would pat her on the head like a good little daughter —which was exactly what he did.

"Where shall we have lunch?" he asked.

She suggested the patients' dining room, since there was a vacant place at her table.

The dining room was an immense hall filled with tables and people. Jakub and Olga sat down and then had to wait a long time before the waitress served them soup. Two other people were sitting at their table. They assumed at once that Jakub was a fellow patient and began to chat with him. Jakub's conversation with Olga was therefore limited to a few quick questions of a practical nature: How did she like the food at the spa; was she satisfied with her doctor; was she satisfied with the treatment? When he asked about her living accommodations, she replied that she had an awful neighbor. She motioned with her head toward Ruzena, who was sitting nearby.

Jakub's two table companions at last got up and took their leave. Jakub said, looking at Ruzena: "Hegel has an interesting observation about the so-called Grecian profile, in which the nose and forehead are joined in a single straight line. According to Hegel, the beauty of such a profile comes from the resulting emphasis on the upper part of the head, which is the seat of intellect and spirit. I was watching your neighbor and it seems to me that in contrast to the Greeks, her whole face is concentrated on her mouth. Look how she's absorbed in chewing, while talking at the top of her voice at the same time. Such emphasis on the lower, animal part of the face would disgust Hegel—and yet even though something about this woman irritates me, I must say she's quite attractive."

"You really think so?" said Olga, her voice betraying annoyance.

Jakub said quickly: "But I'd be scared of that mouth. I'd be scared it might gobble me up." And he added: "Hegel could find nothing wrong with you, though. The dominant part of your face is your forehead, which immediately lets everyone know how intelligent you are."

"Ideas of this kind always get on my nerves," said Olga sharply. "They imply that a person's physiognomy is a picture of their spirit. But that's absolute nonsense. I picture my soul with a big chin and a sensuous mouth, yet my actual chin is small and my mouth is small, too. If I had never seen myself in a mirror and had to describe my appearance by the way I know myself from the inside, the picture wouldn't at all look like me! I am not at all the person I look like!"

4

It would be difficult to find an appropriate word to describe Jakub's relationship to Olga. She was the daughter of a friend who had been executed when Olga was seven years old. Jakub decided at that time to keep the orphaned girl under his wing. He had no children and was attracted by the idea of entering into a kind of obligation-free fatherhood. Jokingly he called her his ward.

They were now sitting in Olga's room. Olga put a pot of water to heat on an electric plate, and Jakub realized how difficult it would be for him to reveal to her the reason for his visit. Every time he was about to tell her that he had come to say goodbye, he became afraid lest such an announcement sound too pathetic and create an inappropriately emotional atmosphere. He had long suspected her of harboring a secret love for him.

Olga pulled two cups out of the cupboard, put a spoonful of instant coffee into each, and poured in boiling water. Jakub dropped in a cube of sugar and slowly stirred it. He heard Olga say: "Tell me something, Jakub. What was my father really like?"

"Why do you ask?"

"Was his conscience really clear?"

"What in the world are you talking about?" asked Jakub. Olga's father had been publicly rehabilitated quite some time earlier, and his death sentence had been declared unjust. Nobody doubted his innocence.

"I didn't mean it that way," said Olga. "Actually, I meant the opposite."

"I don't understand."

"I was wondering whether he hadn't done to other people exactly the same thing as was done to him. After all, the people who drove him to the gallows were his kind: they had the same beliefs, they were the same fanatics. They were convinced that every opinion that dissented—no matter how slightly—was a deadly threat to the revolution. They were morbidly mistrustful. They sent him to his death in the name of a holy dogma which he professed himself. Why then are you so sure he was innocent of having done the same thing to others?"

Jakub hesitated. "Time flies so fast, and the past is becoming harder and harder to understand," he said at last. "What do you know of your father besides a few letters, a few pages of his diary which they were kind enough to return to you, and a few memories from his friends?"

"Why are you avoiding the question?" insisted Olga. "I asked you very clearly: Was my father the same kind of person as those who condemned him to death?"

Jakub shrugged. "Perhaps."

"Then why couldn't he have been capable of committing the same cruelties?"

"Theoretically speaking," Jakub said slowly and deliberately, "theoretically speaking, it is possible he had perpetrated the same kind of injustice as was done to him. There isn't a person on this planet who is not capable of sending a fellow human being to death without any great pangs of conscience. At least I have never found anyone like that. If humanity ever changes in that regard, it will lose one of its most basic characteristics. Those will no longer be human beings, but creatures of some other type."

"I just love the attitude you people have!" Olga burst out as if addressing thousands of Jakubs. "By turning all of humanity into murderers, your own murders cease to be crimes and become an essential characteristic of the human race!"

"The majority of people lead their existence within a small, idyllic circle bounded by their family, their home, and their work," replied Jakub. "They live in a secure realm somewhere between good and evil. They are sincerely horrified by the sight of a killer. And yet all you have to do is remove them from this peaceful circle and they, too, turn into murderers, without quite knowing how it happened.

Every now and again history exposes humans to certain pressures and traps which nobody can resist. But what's the use of talking about it? It makes no difference to you what your father was theoretically capable of doing, and there is no way of proving it anyway. The only thing you need to concern yourself about is what he actually did or did not do. And in that respect his conscience was clear."

"Are you absolutely sure about that?"

"Absolutely. Nobody knew him better than I."

"I am really relieved to hear you say that," Olga said. "You know, I didn't ask you these things without good reason. I have been getting anonymous letters for some time. They say I have no right to play the daughter of a martyr, because my father was responsible for persecuting plenty of innocent people whose only crime was that their idea about the world was different from his."

"Nonsense," Jakub said.

"They describe my father as a violent fanatic and cruel man. Those letters are anonymous and ugly, but they are not vulgar. The writers express themselves without exaggeration, concretely and precisely, so that I almost found myself believing them."

"It's all just one endless chain of revenge," said Jakub. "I'll tell you something. When your father was arrested the jails were full of people who had been rounded up during the first wave of revolutionary enthusiasm. Your father was recognized as a well-known communist politician, and at the first opportunity the inmates fell upon him and beat him unconscious. The guards watched with malicious smiles on their faces."

"I know," Olga replied, and Jakub realized that she had heard this story many times before. He had made up his mind long ago to stop talking about these things, but it didn't work. It was as difficult as asking someone who has experienced a bad automobile crash to stop thinking about it.

"I know," Olga repeated. "But all the same, I don't blame those prisoners. They were jailed without any trial, often for no reason at all. And suddenly they were standing face to face with one whom they considered responsible for their plight."

"The moment your father put on his prison uniform he became one of them. There was no sense in attacking him, especially in front of the amused guards. It was nothing but cowardly revenge. A base impulse to kick a helpless victim. And the letters you're getting stem from the same kind of thirst for revenge, which as I now realize, is stronger than time."

"Listen, Jakub. One hundred thousand people were put in prison! Thousands never came back! And nobody responsible for this injustice ever seems to have been punished! This thirst for revenge, as you call it, is really just an unsatisfied longing for justice."

"To persecute a daughter because of her father has nothing to do with justice. Just remember how you had to leave your home, move out of your home town, give up your studies—all because of your father. A dead father, whom you barely knew! And now for the sake of your father you are to be persecuted by the other side as well? I'll tell you the saddest discovery of my life: The victims are no better than their oppressors. I can easily imagine the roles reversed. You can call it a kind of alibi-ism, an attempt to evade responsibility and to blame everything on the Creator Who made man the way he is. And maybe it's good that you see things that way. Because to come to the conclusion that there is no difference between the guilty and their victims is to reach a state where you *abandon all hope*. And that, my dear, is a definition of *hell*."

5

Ruzena's two colleagues could hardly wait to find out how her previous day's meeting had turned out, but they were busy all morning in another part of the establishment and it wasn't until about three in the afternoon that they caught up with their friend. They overwhelmed her with questions.

Ruzena faltered and said uncertainly: "He told me that he loved me and that he would marry me."

"You see! Didn't I tell you?" exulted the thin one. "And is he going to get a divorce?"

"He said he would."

"He'll jolly well have to," said the older nurse in a chipper tone. "A baby is a baby. And his wife is childless."

Ruzena had no choice but to tell them the plain truth: "He says he'll take me to Prague. He'll find me a job there. He says we'll go to Italy on a vacation. But he doesn't want us to be saddled with a baby right away. And he's right. The first years are the best, and if we had children right off we wouldn't be able to enjoy each other."

The middle-aged nurse gasped. "What? You want to have it removed?"

Ruzena nodded.

"You're crazy!" the thin one exclaimed.

"He got you drunk on moon-juice!" said the older one. "The moment you get rid of the baby he'll send you packing!"

"Why would he do that?"

"You want to bet?"

"If he loves me?"

"And how do you know he loves you?"

"He said so."

"Then why didn't you hear a peep from him for two months?"

"He was afraid of love."

"How's that again?"

"How can I explain it to you? He was afraid that he was falling in love with me."

"And that's why he kept mum?"

"He wanted to test himself, to see if he could forget me. That's fair enough, isn't it?"

"I see," continued the older one. "And when he found out that he knocked you up, he suddenly realized that he couldn't forget you."

"He says he's glad I'm pregnant. Not because of the baby,

but because he heard from me. That made him realize how much he loves me."

"Good Lord, what a ninny you are!" said the thin one.

"Why do you call me that?"

"Because the baby is all that you have on him," replied the older one. "If you lose that, you'll have nothing and he'll take off."

"I want him to marry me for my own sake and not for the sake of a baby!"

"Who in the world do you think you are? Why in God's name would he marry you for your own sake?"

The agitated conversation went on and on, and both colleagues kept insisting over and over that the baby was Ruzena's trump card, which she must never give up.

"I'd never let them take a baby from me, that I can tell you! Never in a million years!" repeated the thin one.

Ruzena began to feel like a helpless little girl and said (it was the same phrase which a day earlier had restored Klima's zest for life): "Then tell me what I should do!"

"Stick to your guns!" said the older nurse. She opened a drawer and handed Ruzena a tube with tablets. "Here, take one! You're all nerves. This will calm you down."

Ruzena put a tablet in her mouth and swallowed it.

"You keep the tube. The dosage is three a day, but you use them only when you need something to settle your nerves. When people are all excited they're liable to do something stupid. Don't forget that he's a sly old fox. He's lived through plenty. But this time his tricks won't work!"

Once again Ruzena was confused and didn't know what to do. A while back she had been sure that her mind was made up, but her friends' arguments sounded so convincing they unsettled her. She walked away full of confusion.

When she reached the downstairs vestibule, an excited young man with a flushed face rushed toward her.

She frowned. "I've told you a hundred times never to wait for me down here. Anyway, after your little performance yesterday

I'm surprised you have the nerve to show your face at all."

"Please don't be angry with me!" pleaded the youth.

"Shush!" she hissed at him. "Now you're going to make a scene here, too, I suppose." She turned to go.

"Then stay and talk to me, if you don't want a scene!"

She had no choice. Patients were passing all around and every once in a while a white-coated nurse or doctor walked by. Ruzena did not want to attract attention; she was thus forced to stay and to assume a casual expression.

"What is it you want?" she whispered.

"Nothing. I just wanted to ask you to forgive me. I'm really sorry for what I've done. But swear to me there is nothing between you and him."

"I've already told you there's nothing between us."

"Then swear."

"Don't be an ass. I don't believe in swearing about such stupid things."

"Because there is something between you!"

"I have already told you there isn't. If you don't take my word for it we've got nothing to talk about. He's simply an old friend. I suppose there isn't anything wrong with having friends? I respect him. I feel very honored to have made his acquaintance."

"I understand. I'm not reproaching you," said the youth.

"Tomorrow he's giving a concert here. I hope you're not going to spy on me again."

"I won't if you give me your solemn word there is nothing between you."

"How many times do I have to tell you that it's beneath my dignity to swear about such things? But I give you my solemn word that if you keep up your snooping, I'll never talk to you again as long as I live."

"Ruzena, it's all because I love you," said the young man plaintively.

"I love you too," Ruzena said in a matter-of-fact way, "but that doesn't mean I make scenes in the middle of a highway."

"You don't love me. You are ashamed of me."

"Nonsense."

"You never want me to be around, you don't want me to go with you anywhere. . . ."

"Shush!" she hissed once again, because he had raised his voice. "My father would kill me if he caught us carrying on. I told you he watched me like a hawk. But now I really must go."

The young man grasped her hand. "Don't go yet!"

Ruzena turned her eyes toward the ceiling in desperation.

The young man said: "Everything would be different if we got married. Your father couldn't stop us. We'd have a family."

"I don't want a family," Ruzena said sharply. "I'd kill myself before I'd have a baby!"

"Why?"

"Because. I don't want any babies."

"I love you, Ruzena," the young man repeated.

And Ruzena said: "And that's why you're trying to drive me to suicide, right?"

"Suicide?" he asked, startled.

"Yes, suicide."

"Ruzena!"

"You'll drive me to suicide. Mark my words! You'll drive me to it for sure!"

"Can I come see you this evening?" he asked humbly.

"No, not tonight," she answered. Then she realized the need to calm him down, and added more softly: "But you can call me another time, Franta. After Sunday." She turned to go.

"Wait," said the young man. "I brought you something. To make up." He handed her a small package.

She took it and strode off.

6

"Is Dr. Skreta really such a strange bird as he pretends to be?"

"I've been wondering that myself for as long as I've known him," answered Jakub.

"Eccentrics don't live too badly if they succeed in convincing people to respect their eccentricity," said Olga. "Dr. Skreta is fantastically absentminded. In the middle of a conversation he suddenly forgets what he was talking about. He stops in the street to chat with somebody and before he knows what's happening he's two hours behind in his office schedule. Yet nobody dares get angry at him, because the good doctor is an officially acknowledged eccentric and only a vulgarian would deny him the right to be an oddball."

"Eccentric or not, I think he's a good physician."

"He may well be, although all of us have the feeling that the practice of medicine is just a sideline to him, just a necessary nuisance which takes time from his more important projects. Tomorrow, for example, he is going to perform on drums."

"Just a moment," interrupted Jakub. "Are you quite sure about that?"

"All I can tell you is that the whole place is plastered with posters announcing tomorrow's concert, featuring the eminent trumpeter Klima with Dr. Skreta performing on drums."

"That's fantastic," remarked Jakub. "Skreta is the biggest daydreamer I have ever known. But his dreams never seem to come true. When I first met him, back in college, Skreta had very little money. He always had very little money, and dreamed of ways to become rich. At that time he had a scheme for breeding terriers, because somebody told him he could sell Welsh terrier pups for four thousand apiece. He had it all figured out. An adult female would produce two litters a year, five pups in each litter. That makes ten a year, ten times four thousand makes forty thousand. Everything was perfectly thought out. He worked hard to get in the good graces of the steward in charge of the student dining room, who promised he'd let the dogs have leftovers from the kitchen. He wrote dissertations for two fellow students in return for a promise that they would walk the dogs for him. No animals were allowed in his dorm, so he kept plying the housemother with candy and flowers until she promised that in his case an exception to the no-dog rule would be made. He went on this way for more than two months, getting everything ready for his dogs, but we all knew that it was just a pipe dream. He needed four thousand to buy the terrier bitch, and nobody lent him the money. Nobody took him seriously. Everybody regarded him as a dreamer, a man with extraordinary talents and initiative, but only for fantasy."

"That's all very touching, but I still don't understand your strange affection for him. He is not even a responsible person. He is never anywhere on time, and what he promises today he'll forget tomorrow."

"That's not quite fair. Actually, he once did me a great favor. Nobody ever performed a more profound service for me in my life."

Jakub reached into his vest pocket and pulled out a folded piece of tissue paper. He carefully unwrapped it. It contained a pale blue pill.

"What is it?" asked Olga.

"Poison."

For a few moments Jakub savored the girl's inquisitive silence, and then continued: "I've had it for more than fifteen years. There was one thing I had learned after a year in prison: A prisoner needs at least this one certainty—that he is master of his own death, capable of choosing its time and manner. When you have that certainty, you can stand almost anything. You always know it is in your power to escape life anytime you choose."

"You had this pill with you in prison?"

"Unfortunately not, but I procured it as soon as I got out."

"But then you no longer needed it!"

"In this country you never know when such a need might arise. Besides, it was a matter of principle with me. I believe that every person should be given a poison tablet on the day he or she reaches maturity. A solemn ceremony should accompany this presentation. Not in order to lure people to suicide. On the contrary, to let them live in greater peace and security. To let everybody live with the certainty that they are lords and masters of their own life and death."

"And how did you manage to get it?"

"Skreta started out as a biochemist in a lab. First I asked somebody else, but he considered it his moral duty to turn me down. Skreta produced the pill for me without the slightest hesitation."

"Probably out of sheer eccentricity."

"Perhaps. But mainly because he understood me. He knew that I was not a hysteric playing suicidal games. He understood my reasoning. I want to return the pill to him today. I won't need it anymore."

"All danger has passed?"

"Tomorrow morning I am leaving this country for good. I have been invited to teach at a foreign university and our government has given me permission to leave."

It was out at last. Jakub looked at Olga and saw that she was smiling. She took him by the hand. "Really? That's marvelous! I'm so happy for you!"

She was expressing the kind of unselfish joy which he would feel if he heard that Olga was leaving for some wonderful place where she could expect to be happy. That surprised him, for he had always feared that she was tied to him—emotionally attached. He was glad to learn that this was not so, but at the same time he was somewhat piqued.

Olga was so absorbed by Jakub's news that she lost interest in the pale blue pill lying on the table between them on a piece of crumpled tissue paper. She made Jakub tell her in detail all the circumstances of his new career.

"I'm so happy that you managed to pull it off. Here, you'd

be considered a suspect character for the rest of your life. You're even barred from working in your own field. And yet they are always preaching to us the glories of loving our native land. How can you love a country that doesn't permit you to work? I'll tell you quite honestly—I don't feel any love for our country. Is that wrong of me?"

"I don't know," replied Jakub. "I really don't. I must admit that I myself have always had a special feeling for this land."

"Maybe it's wrong," Olga continued, "but I don't feel any ties at all. What kind of ties could I have here?"

"Even sad memories create a kind of attachment."

"Attachment to what? To moon over a certain place just because one happened to have been born there? I can't understand how people can talk about freedom and yet remain shackled to such a weight. After all, roots are of no use to a tree if the soil is barren; a tree finds its real native soil only where there is moisture to nourish it."

"And how about you? Do you have the moisture you need?"

"In general, yes. Now that they have at last given me permission to study, I am content. I will pursue my science and the rest doesn't interest me. I didn't create the present circumstances and I am not responsible for them. But tell me, when are you actually leaving?"

"Tomorrow."

"So soon?" She clutched his arm. "Please! If you were so nice and came all the way here to say goodbye to me, couldn't you stay just a little longer?"

Everything was different from what he had expected. She was behaving neither like a girl who was secretly in love with him nor like a ward who was showing daughterlike affection. She held his hand tenderly and expressively, gazed into his eyes, and repeated: "Don't rush away! It would be a pity if you just said goodbye and that was that."

Jakub was taken aback. "We'll see," he said. "Skreta is also trying to talk me into staying longer."

"You must stay," said Olga. "We have so little time for each other. Now I am again due for my treatment." She paused, and then announced her decision to skip treatment and stay with Jakub.

"No, no, you can't do that. Your health comes first," said Jakub. "I'll walk over with you."

"That's fine," said Olga happily. She opened her closet and rummaged around for something.

The pale blue pill was still lying on the table. Olga, the only person to whom Jakub had ever confided his secret about it, was standing with her back to it, peering into the closet. It occurred to Jakub that the pale blue pill somehow symbolized the drama of his life, a forlorn, forgotten, and probably rather uninteresting drama. He told himself it was high time to end this uninteresting story, to write *finis* to it quickly and leave it behind. He folded the pill once more in its tissue wrapper and stuck it in his pocket.

Olga pulled a large handbag out of the closet, dropped in a folded towel, closed the closet door and said to Jakub: "Let's go!"

7

God only knows how long Ruzena had been sitting in the park. She seemed glued to the bench, perhaps because her thoughts, too, were hopelessly stuck.

Only yesterday she had still believed the trumpeter. Not only because his story was agreeable, but because believing him was the simplest way out: with a clear conscience she could withdraw from a contest that was beyond her strength. But now that her colleagues had ridiculed her gullibility, she began to mistrust him again and she thought about him with hatred; deep down in her soul she suspected that she was neither clever nor persistent enough to win him.

Listlessly she tore open the package Franta had given her. It contained something made of pale blue material, and Ruzena guessed that it was a nightgown. A nightgown in which he would love to see her, night after night, all the nights of her life. She gazed at the material until it seemed to dissolve into a blue lake, a sticky lake of love, a blue quagmire of goodness and devotion.

Whom did she hate more? The man who didn't want her or the man who pined for her?

And so she sat on the bench, paralyzed by her two hates, totally unaware of what was happening around her. A van pulled up to the curb, followed by a small green truck from which emanated the sound of furious howling and barking. The door of the van opened and out stepped an elderly man with a red band around his sleeve. Ruzena looked at him dully, without comprehending.

The man shouted some sort of order and a second man stepped out of the vehicle, also elderly and also sporting a red band on his sleeve. He was holding a long pole with a wire loop attached to one end. One by one, more men got out, all equipped with red bands and long, looped poles.

The man who had emerged first shouted more orders, and the bizarre company of lancers alternated "at attention" and "at ease." Then the leader rasped out an order and the men trotted into the park. There they broke ranks, with each one going off in a separate direction, some jogging along paths, others crossing lawns. The park was full of strolling adults and playing children. Everybody stopped in amazement to watch the old gentlemen charging with poles cocked.

Ruzena, too, watched the proceedings, having at last roused herself out of her melancholy ruminations. She recognized her father among the red-banded troop; she looked on with vague distaste but without particular surprise.

A little dog was frisking around a birch tree in the middle of the lawn. One of the elderly gentlemen started running toward him. The dog stopped and watched in surprise. The man stretched the pole as far as he could, trying to slip the wire noose over the dog's head. But the pole was long, the old arms weak, and the frustrated oldster could not hit the mark. The wire loop swayed uncertainly over the dog's head, while the animal watched intently.

In the meantime, another red-banded gentleman was rushing to the aid of his colleague; his arms were stronger, and the dog soon found himself in the wire collar. The old man yanked the pole, the wire cut into the hairy neck, and the dog let out a howl. Both gentlemen laughed, dragging the dog across the lawn toward the parked vehicles. They opened the large door of the van, releasing a mighty wave of barking, then threw the dog inside and slammed the door shut.

Ruzena witnessed everything, but she perceived it only as a reflection of her own unhappy story: she was a woman caught between two realms. Klima's world rejected her, while the world she wanted to flee (Franta's world of banality, boredom, failure, and capitulation) pursued her like this relentless squad, as if she, too, were about to be dragged off in a wire noose.

A boy of about twelve was standing on the sandy path, desperately calling his dog, which had wandered off into the bushes. Instead of the dog, however, out of the shrubbery emerged Ruzena's father carrying a pole. The boy fell silent at once; he was afraid to call the dog because he knew that the old man would drag him away. He therefore scampered down the path to get away from the pursuer, but the old man jogged right after him. They were running side by side, Ruzena's pole-carrying father and the boy, who began to cry, then turned and started running back. Ruzena's father did likewise. Once more they were side by side.

A dachshund ambled out of the bushes. Ruzena's father stretched the pole toward him, but the dog avoided the noose and ran up to the boy, who lifted him up and pressed him in his arms. Other members of the squad came to the aid of Ruzena's father and dragged the dachshund out of the boy's arms. The boy was sobbing, shouting, and thrashing about. The old men had to pin back his arms and cover his mouth, for the shouting was attracting the attention of passersby who turned to look but dared not interfere.

Ruzena was fed up with watching her father and his comrades. But where could she go? There was nothing to entertain her in her room except a half-finished detective story that did not entice her at all; the movie theater was showing a film she had already seen, and the most exciting prospect the lobby of Richmond House had to offer was an old TV set. She decided in favor of television, and got up. The shouting of the old men, which resounded from all sides, made her once more intensely conscious of the quiet, precious life budding inside her. It seemed like something holy, something that transformed and uplifted her. It distinguished her from those foolish fanatics chasing dogs. She began to feel convinced that she must not give up, she must not capitulate, for she was carrying in her womb her only hope, her only passport to the future.

When she reached the edge of the park she noticed Jakub. He was standing on the sidewalk in front of Richmond House, watching the dog roundup. She had seen him only once before, at lunch a few hours earlier, but she remembered him. Ruzena greatly disliked the patient who had been living next door to her, and who had been in the habit of banging on the wall whenever the volume of the radio was up ever so slightly. Ruzena therefore followed everything which concerned her former neighbor with keen animosity.

She disliked this man's face. It looked ironic to her, and she hated irony. It had always seemed to her that irony—all irony—was like an armed watchman guarding the portal to her future, scrutinizing her and disdainfully refusing her admittance. Head held high, shoulders back, she intended to pass Jakub arrayed in all the seductive splendor of her bosom and the pride of her sprouting belly.

Suddenly the man (she was watching him out of the corner of her eye) said in a calm, gentle voice: "Come here . . . come on, come over here. . . ."

At first she did not understand why he was calling her. She was confused by the tenderness in his voice and she didn't know how to answer. But then she turned around and saw that a fat bulldog with an ugly human face was following right on her heels.

The dog responded to Jakub's voice and came toward him. Jakub took him by the collar. "Come along with me or you'll be in bad trouble." The dog lifted his trusting head toward the man, his tongue waving like a gay little flag.

It was an instant of humiliation, ridiculous and trivial, yet unmistakable: he had paid no attention to her seductiveness nor to her pride. She had thought he was addressing her, and instead he had been talking to a dog. She walked by him and stopped at the stairs in front of Richmond House.

From across the street two old men came rushing at Jakub. She watched with malicious anticipation, unable to prevent herself from siding with the oldsters.

While one old man shouted: "Release that animal at once!" Jakub led the dog by the collar to the stairway of the building. The other old man added: "In the name of the law!"

Jakub ignored them and kept on going. One of the poles, however, was extended from behind him, almost touching the side of his body, the wire loop bobbing tentatively over the bulldog's head. Jakub grabbed the pole and threw it to the ground.

A third old man came running up. He shouted: "You're interfering with official business! I'll call the police!"

Another oldster complained in a piping voice: "He was running wild all over the park! He was in the playground where dogs are prohibited! He pissed on the sand in the sandbox! Which comes first, children or dogs?"

Ruzena was looking down on this scene from the head of the stairs and the pride which until now she had felt only in her belly, began to swell throughout her body, filling her with a defiant strength. As Jakub climbed the stairs toward her, she said: "That dog has no business here!"

Jakub answered mildly, but she could no longer retreat. Straddling the wide doorway of Richmond House, she repeated: "This building is for patients and not for dogs. Dogs are not permitted here."

"Where are your pole and your noose, miss?" said Jakub, trying to shove his way past her, the dog in his arms.

Ruzena heard the irony in Jakub's remark—that hateful irony which always seemed to be kicking her back where she had come from, where she did not want to stay. Her eyes blazed with anger. She grasped the dog by the collar. Now they were both tugging at the collar, Jakub pulling one way and she pulling back.

Jakub grabbed Ruzena's wrist and yanked her hand free with such violence that the girl staggered.

"I'll bet you're the type that fills baby carriages with dogs!" she shouted after him.

Jakub turned around, and their eyes met with the clash of sudden, naked hatred.

8

The bulldog sniffed inquisitively around the room, as if unaware of having just narrowly escaped from mortal peril. Jakub stretched out on the couch, wondering what to do with the dog. He liked him, he seemed to be a good-natured, cheerful animal. Actually, the nonchalance shown by the dog in making himself so quickly at home in a strange room and in trusting a strange man bordered on stupidity. After investigating all four corners of the room, he jumped up on the couch and lay down next to Jakub. Jakub was startled, but accepted this manifestation of comradeship without resistance. He put his arm on the dog's back and enjoyed the warmth emanating from the animal's body. He had always liked dogs. They were affectionate, cuddlesome, devoted, and at the same time totally unfathomable. Man will never know what actually goes on in the heads and hearts of these trusting, merry ambassadors from the strange, incomprehensible world of nature.

He scratched the dog's back and pondered the scene he had witnessed earlier. The old men with long poles he equated with prison guards, inquisitors and informers who snoop on their neighbors in the hope of catching a stray political remark. What motivated such people to do their deplorable work? Anger? Certainly. But also the longing for order, a desire to turn the human world into an inorganic one, where everything would function perfectly and work on schedule, subordinated to a suprapersonal system. The longing for order is at the same time a longing for death, because life is an incessant disruption of order. Or to put it the other way around: the desire for order is a virtuous pretext, an excuse for virulent misanthropy.

Then he recalled the fair-haired girl who had tried to block his way, and he felt an aching surge of hate. He was not angry at the old men with poles, he knew their ilk, he never doubted that such types existed, that they had to exist, and that they would forever be his persecutors. But that girl, she was a different story. She represented his eternal downfall. She was pretty, and appeared on the scene not as a persecutor but as a spectator lured by the show and identifying with the persecutors. Jakub was always horrified by the readiness of bystanders to rush to the executioner's aid and obligingly help pin down the victim. In the course of time the executioner had grown into a familiar, folksy kind of figure, while the victims still had an unpleasantly aristocratic smell about them. The soul of the crowd, which perhaps had once identified with the poor victim, now identifies with the poor persecutor. In our century, the hunt on human beings is a hunt on the privileged: those who read books or own dogs.

His hand felt the warm canine body, and he told himself that the fair-haired girl was an omen, the bearer of an arcane message signifying that he was destined never to be accepted in this land and she—the people's ambassador—would always gladly deliver him into the hands of men with snare-tipped poles. He embraced the dog and pressed him close. The thought crossed his mind that he must not leave the animal behind, defenseless, that he should take him abroad as a souvenir of persecution, as one of those who had escaped. But then he realized that he was sheltering this good-natured mutt as if he were a desperate fugitive, and suddenly it all seemed ludicrous.

There was a knock on the door and Skreta entered. "It's high time you're home. I've been looking for you all afternoon. Where have you been?"

"I was with Olga, and then . . ." He was about to launch into the story of the dog, but Skreta interrupted:

"I might have known. You're wasting time, and we've got so much to go over. I told Bartleff that you're here and he's invited us both over to his apartment."

At that moment the dog jumped off the couch, walked up to Skreta, stood up on his hind legs, and placed his front paws on the doctor's chest. Skreta rubbed the back of the dog's neck and without surprise said: "Hello, Bobis, hello there, there's a good dog. . . ."

"That's Bobis?"

"Yes," answered Skreta, explaining that the dog belonged to the owners of a nearby inn and everybody in the vicinity knew him because he loved to roam.

The dog realized that he was the subject of conversation and was pleased. He wagged his tail and tried to lick Skreta's face.

Dr. Skreta said: "You're an excellent psychologist. You have to analyze Bartleff for me. I don't know how to approach him, and I have great plans for the two of us."

"You mean those holy pictures?"

"To hell with holy pictures," said Skreta. "I've got more important projects in mind. I want him to adopt me."

"To adopt you?"

"To adopt me as a son. It's an extremely important matter for me. If I became his son I'd automatically get American citizenship."

"You want to emigrate?"

"No, I don't. I'm in the middle of far-reaching experiments and I don't want to interrupt them. That's another thing I want to talk to you about today, because I need your help in those experiments. As far as American citizenship is concerned, the point is that I'd get an American passport and I could travel freely all over the world. If you're just an ordinary citizen of this our country, you're stuck here forever. And I'm dying to visit Iceland."

"Why Iceland of all places?"

"Because that's the best place for catching salmon," explained Skreta, and continued: "There is one small complication, namely that Bartleff is only seven years older than I am. I'll have to explain to him that adoption is strictly a legal affair which has nothing to do with natural paternity and that from a theoretical viewpoint he could be my adoptive father even if he were younger than I. I hope he'll understand, although he has an awfully young wife. A patient of mine. She is due to arrive here day after tomorrow. I sent Kveta to the city to meet her at the airport."

"Kveta knows of your scheme?"

"Of course. I told her that at all costs she must try to get into the good graces of her future mother-in-law."

"And what about the American? How does he feel about your proposal?"

"I can't figure him out. He doesn't seem to get the idea at all. That's why I need you, to find out what makes him tick so I can approach him the right way."

Skreta glanced at his watch and said that Bartleff was waiting.

"But what about Bobis?"

"What's he doing here, anyway?"

Jakub explained to his friend how he had saved the dog's life, but Skreta was immersed in his own thoughts and was only half listening. After Jakub had finished, he said: "The innkeeper's wife is one of my patients. Two years ago she gave birth to a beautiful baby. They are very fond of Bobis, you should really bring him out there tomorrow. In the meantime we'll give him a sleeping pill so he doesn't bother us."

He took a tube out of his pocket and shook a tablet into the palm of his hand. He took hold of the dog, opened his jaws, and dropped the tablet down his throat.

"He'll soon be having sweet dreams," he said, and led Jakub out of the room.

9

Bartleff greeted his two guests, and Jakub looked around the room. He stepped up to the painting of the bearded saint. "I understand you're a painter," he said to Bartleff.

"Yes. That's Saint Lazarus, my patron saint."

"Why did you paint his halo blue?" Jakub inquired.

"I am glad you asked. People generally look at a picture without having the slightest idea what they're seeing. I painted the halo blue simply because in reality halos are blue."

Jakub showed surprise and Bartleff continued: "People who love God with exceptional fervor are rewarded by a joy which fills their souls and radiates outward. The light of this divine joy is mild and calm, and has the color of the blue heavens."

"Let me understand you," interrupted Jakub. "Do you actually believe that halos are more than graphic symbols?"

"Certainly," Bartleff replied. "Naturally, I don't imagine that they shine continuously or that saints walk around the world like marching lampposts. Of course not. Only at certain moments of intense inner joy do they radiate a bluish glow. In the first centuries after the death of Jesus, when there were many saints and many people who knew them intimately, there was universal agreement about the color of halos, and you'll find them blue on all paintings and frescoes of that time. It's only since the fifth century that painters gradually began to depict halos in other colors, such as orange or yellow. By the Gothic era, they were invariably shown in gold. Gold was more decorative and better expressed the secular power and glory of the Church. But it had no more resemblance to a real halo than the church of that time resembled original Christianity."

"That's interesting," said Jakub, while Bartleff walked over to the liquor cabinet and asked his guests what they wanted to drink.

Everyone settled on cognac, and Bartleff turned to Dr. Skreta: "I hope you won't forget about that unfortunate father. It's very important to me."

Skreta assured his host that everything would turn out all right, at which point Jakub asked what they were referring to. After the subject of the conversation had been explained to him (let us pay tribute to the chivalrous discretion of the two men: no names were mentioned at all), Jakub expressed compassion for the anonymous impregnator.

"Who among us has not experienced this martyrdom! It is one of life's trials. Those who succumb and become fathers against their will suffer lifelong defeat. They turn bitter, like all losers, and wish the same fate on others."

"My dear friend!" exclaimed Bartleff. "How can you talk this way in front of a happy father? If you stay another two or three days you'll have an opportunity to see my splendid son and you'll take back what you just said!"

"I won't take it back," said Jakub, "because you did not become a father against your will!"

"That is the gospel truth. I am a father by my own will and by the will of Dr. Skreta."

Skreta nodded in satisfaction and declared that he too had an entirely different opinion on paternity from Jakub, as evidenced by the happy fecundity of his wife, Kveta. He added: "The only thing that makes me somewhat skeptical regarding human procreation is the unintelligent selection of parents. Some of the most unattractive individuals in the world feel that they must multiply at all costs. They are apparently under the illusion that the burden of ugliness becomes lighter if it is shared with descendants."

Bartleff characterized Dr. Skreta's viewpoint as aesthetic racism: "Let's not forget that Socrates was ugly as sin, and that many famous lovers fell short of physical perfection. Aesthetic racism is almost always a manifestation of inexperience. People who haven't delved very deeply into the world of amorous delights judge women strictly on the basis of surface appearance. But those who really know women realize that our eyes can reveal to us only a tiny fragment of the treasures which a woman can bestow. When God bade mankind to love one another and multiply, Dr. Skreta, God meant the homely as well as the beautiful. In any case, I am convinced that the aesthetic criterion comes from the devil and not from God. In paradise, no distinction existed between ugliness and beauty."

Then Jakub entered the discussion, maintaining that aesthetic considerations played no part in his distaste for parenthood: "But I can cite ten other reasons against paternity," he added.

"Go on, I am curious," Bartleff said.

"First of all, I don't like motherhood," said Jakub, pausing pensively. "The modern age has unmasked all myths. Childhood has long ceased to be an age of innocence. Freud discovered infant sexuality and told us all about Oedipus. Only Jocasta still remains shrouded, and nobody dares to tear off her veil. Motherhood is the last and greatest taboo, and it is there that the greatest curse is concealed as well. There is no bondage more oppressive than that between mother and child. It cripples the child forever, and a maturing son causes his mother the most cruel erotic suffering. I repeat that motherhood is a curse and I don't wish to propagate it."

"Go on," said Bartleff.

"There is still another reason why I don't want to see mothers multiply," said Jakub somewhat uneasily. "I love the female body, and I am disgusted by the idea of a beloved breast turning into a milk bag."

"Go on," said Bartleff.

"Our doctor here will certainly confirm that women who choose abortion are treated much less sympathetically by the medical staff than women who bear children. Nurses show a certain contempt toward women undergoing abortions, even though they themselves may have to subject themselves to the same procedure at some point in their lives. But the distaste is far stronger than logic, because the cult of fertility is a dictate of nature. That's why it is idle to look for logic in the propaganda for population growth. In the population morality preached by the Church, do you recognize the voice of Jesus? Or do you think that the official communist position on population growth echoes the voice of Marx? The very desire to preserve the species will end up choking it to death. But the propaganda grinds on, and the public is moved to tears by the picture of a nursing mother or a grinning infant. It disgusts me. When I imagine myself bending over a baby carriage with an idiotic smile, like millions of other dizzy daddies, it makes me shudder."

"Go on," said Bartleff.

"And of course I must consider what kind of world I'd be sending my child into. In no time at all he'd be whisked away to school, where his head would be filled with the very lies and nonsense I have tried all my life to combat. Should I watch my descendant slowly growing into a conformist idiot? Or should I bequeath my own intellectual heritage to him, only to watch his mounting frustration as he gets entangled in the same old conflicts?"

"Go on," said Bartleff.

"And then of course I have to think of myself, too. In this country parents are punished for the disobedience of their children, and children for the misdeeds of their parents. How many young people have been thrown out of school beeause their parents fell into disfavor! And how many parents resigned themselves to a lifetime of cowardly submission just to avoid endangering their children! Anybody in this country who wants to keep any freedom at all should forget about having children," Jakub said, and lapsed into silence.

"You've given us only five reasons. You still need five more to make it an even ten," said Bartleff.

"The last reason is so overwhelming that it makes up for five," Jakub retorted. "Parenthood implies absolute affirmation of human life. My fathering a child would be like proclaiming to the world: I was born, I tasted of life, and I found it so good that I deem it worthy to be multiplied."

"And you did not find life to be good?"

Jakub tried to be precise, and said carefully: "All I know is that I could never say with deep conviction: Man is an excellent creature and I want him propagated."

"That's because you have experienced life from only one side, the worst side," said Dr. Skreta. "You've never known how to live. You have always thought it was your duty to be in the thick of it, so to speak. In the center of action. And what was that action that you were so engrossed in? Politics. Politics, the least substantial and least valuable part of life. Politics is the dirty foam on the surface, while real life takes place in the depths. Research on female fertility has been going on for thousands of years. It is a history which is solid, reliable. And it doesn't make a particle of difference which government happens to be in power at the moment. When I put on my rubber glove and touch a woman's womb, I am much closer to the center of life than you, who have almost lost your own life in your concern for human happiness."

Far from protesting against his friend's rebuke, Jakub nodded in agreement. Encouraged, Skreta continued: "Archimedes with his circles, Michelangelo with a piece of stone, Pasteur with his test tubes—these were people who changed human life and made real history, whereas the politicians . . ." Skreta waved contemptuously.

"Whereas the politicians? I'll answer that," said Jakub. "Art and science are the real arenas of history, while politics is actually a closed laboratory for performing novel experiments with human beings. Human guinea pigs are hurled down trapdoors and then lifted up onto the stage, lured by applause and intimidated by the hangman's noose, vilified and forced to vilify others. I was a part of that laboratory, both as a researcher and as an experimental animal. I realize that I have created no new values (and neither have any of my fellow workers), but I do think I have learned more than most people about the nature of man."

"I understand you," said Bartleff, "and I know the laboratory you have been describing, even though my role was never that of a researcher but always that of a guinea pig. The war found me in Germany. The woman I loved denounced me to the Gestapo. They had come to her with a photograph showing me arm in arm with another woman. She was hurt by it, and, as you know, injured love often takes on the guise of hatred. I went to prison with the remarkable feeling that it was love that had put me there. Is it not marvelous to find oneself in the hands of the Gestapo and to realize that this fate is actually the privilege of a passionately loved man?"

Jakub retorted: "The one thing that really disgusts me about humanity is the way human cruelty, baseness, and narrowness so often lie concealed under a veil of lyricism and sentiment. A human being sends you to your death, weeping hot tears over this act of disappointed love. And you go to the gallows for the sake of some perfectly commonplace woman, convinced that you are playing a lofty role in a tragedy worthy of Shakespeare's pen."

"After the war was over she came back to me in tears," continued Bartleff as if he had not heard Jakub's remark. "I told her: Have no fear, Bartleff is not a vindictive man."

"In this connection," said Jakub, "I am often reminded of King Herod. You know the story. He supposedly found out about the birth of the future Jewish king, and, fearful for his throne, he had all the infants killed. My own ideas about Herod are quite different, even though I know it's only a bit of fantasy. I think of Herod as an educated, wise, and noble king, who had spent a long apprenticeship in the laboratory of politics and had learned much about the world and man. Herod realized that man should never have been created. Actually, this doubt was not so unfounded and sinful as it may seem. If I am not mistaken, even the Lord Himself had second thoughts about mankind and entertained the idea of canceling His work of creation."

"That's correct," Bartleff agreed. "It is written in Genesis: 'I will destroy man whom I have created . . . for it repenteth me that I have made them.' "

"Perhaps it was just a moment of weakness on the part of the Lord when He permitted Noah to save himself in the ark, thus allowing the human story to continue. Can we be certain that God never regretted this moment of weakness? But whether He repented or not, it was too late. God cannot make Himself ridiculous by continually reversing His decisions. Perhaps it was God Himself who planted the idea in Herod's mind? Can we rule out such a possibility?"

Bartleff shrugged his shoulders and remained silent.

"Herod was a king. He was not responsible merely for himself. He couldn't very well tell himself, as I do: Let others do as they please, I refuse to propagate the race. Herod was a king and knew that it was up to him to make decisions not only for himself but for many others, and he decided on behalf of all mankind that man would cease repeating himself. This was how the Massacre of the Innocents came about. Herod was not led by the base motives ascribed to him traditionally. Herod was animated by the noblest longing to liberate the world from the clutches of mankind."

"I rather like your interpretation of Herod," said Bartleff. "In fact, I like it so much that from now on I will think of the Massacre of the Innocents the same way you do. But don't forget that at the very time Herod decided to do away with mankind, a little boy was born in Bethlehem who eluded his knife. And this boy grew up and told people that only one thing was needed to make life worthwhile: to love one another. Perhaps Herod was better educated and more experienced. Jesus was actually a young man, and probably knew little about life. Maybe all his teaching can be explained by his youth and inexperience. His naïveté, if you like. And yet he was right."

"Right? Who has proved him right?" asked Jakub belligerently.

"Nobody," replied Bartleff. "Nobody has proved it, and nobody ever will. Jesus loved his Father so much that he could not bear to see His handiwork turn out badly. He was led by love, not by reason. That's why the dispute between Herod and Jesus can be decided only within our hearts. Is it worthwhile to be a human being or not? I have no proof, but I believe with Jesus that the answer is yes." With a smile, he pointed his finger at Dr. Skreta. "That's why I sent my wife here, to our good doctor, who is in my eyes one of Jesus's holy disciples, for he knows how to perform miracles and how to wake the slumbering wombs of women to new life. I drink to his health!"

10

Jakub had always treated Olga with paternal solicitude and liked to refer to himself as her "old gent." She knew that there were many women in his life with whom he acted entirely differently, and she was jealous. But today, for the first time, it occurred to her that there really was something old about Jakub. His behavior exuded that faint aroma of mustiness which young people recognize in their elders.

It is characteristic of aging gentlemen to brag about the hardships they have endured, and to convert their tormented past into a kind of museum of fortitude (alas, these sad museums generally attract so few visitors!).

Olga recognized that she was one of the main living exhibits of Jakub's museum, and that his nobly unselfish relationship to her was meant to move visitors to tears.

Today, she had been introduced to the most precious nonliving exhibit of the museum: the pale blue pill. When he had unwrapped it in front of her earlier in the day she had been surprised to find that she wasn't the least bit moved. She understood that Jakub had gone through terrible ordeals and had seriously considered suicide, but the pathos with which he recounted his experiences seemed ridiculous. His way of carefully folding back the tissue paper seemed contrived, too, as if he were bringing to light a priceless diamond. And she could not understand why he was so determined to return the poison, since he took such pains in proclaiming that every adult should have control of his own death under all circumstances. After leaving the country he might fall victim to cancer or some other dread disease and still have need of the poison. No. It was quite evident that for Jakub the pill was not simply a useful expedient, but a sacred symbol which must be ritually returned to the high priest. And that was absurd.

She was on her way back from the baths, heading toward Richmond House. In spite of all her malicious thoughts, she was looking forward to being with Jakub. She had a great desire to desecrate his museum and to behave like a woman rather than an exhibit. She was therefore somewhat disappointed to find a note on the door telling her that Jakub and Skreta were next door at Bartleff's apartment and asking her to meet them there. She tended to be uneasy in company; she did not know Bartleff at all, and Dr. Skreta generally treated her with an air of benevolent indifference.

However, Bartleff quickly put her at ease. He greeted her with a deep bow, and chided Dr. Skreta for not having introduced such an interesting woman to him sooner.

Skreta retorted that Jakub had entrusted the girl to his care, and that he had deliberately refrained from introducing her to Bartleff because he knew that no woman could resist him.

Bartleff accepted this excuse with cheerful satisfaction. He lifted the telephone and placed an order for dinner.

"It is unbelievable," said Dr. Skreta, "how our friend is managing to live so well in this backwater where there isn't one single inn that serves a passable meal."

Bartleff ran his hand through an open cigar box standing next to the phone, which was full of silver American half-dollars. "One must be generous. . . ." He smiled.

Jakub remarked that he had never known a man like Bartleff, who believed so passionately in God and yet just as passionately managed to enjoy the good life.

"This shows that you have probably never known any real Christians," said Bartleff. "The word *evangel* means 'glad tidings.' The enjoyment of life is the most fundamental legacy of Jesus."

It seemed to Olga that this was a good point for her to enter the conversation. "My teachers always stressed that Christians regarded earthly existence only as a vale of tears and eagerly anticipated the real life which would begin only after death."

"My dear young lady," Bartleff said, "never trust teachers."

"And we were taught that the principal task of saints was the renunciation of life," continued Olga. "Instead of loving one another they scourged themselves, instead of conversing with one another they shut themselves up in monasteries, and instead of ordering dinner by telephone they chewed roots and berries."

"You don't understand saints at all, dear Olga. They were people with an enormous desire for the joys of life, only they reached these joys by special ways. What do you think is the highest pleasure a human being can attain? You could not even guess at the answer, for you are not sufficiently sincere. This is not a reproach, for sincerity necessitates self-understanding and self-understanding necessitates a certain maturity. So how could a girl who radiates youthfulness be sincere? She can't, for she does not know her inner self. But if she did know herself, she would agree with me that the greatest human pleasure is being admired."

Olga replied that she could think of greater pleasures.

"I don't believe so," said Bartleff. "Take that famous sprinter who's been so much in the news lately, the one who won three Olympic races in a row. Do you think of him as someone who has abjured life? And yet he undoubtedly had to renounce much pleasant chatting, lovemaking, and feasting to run around a practice track for hours and hours, day after day. The training routine of an athlete bears a great resemblance to the regime of our saints. Saint Makarios of Alexandria, when he was living in the desert, regularly filled a basket with sand, put it on his back, and trudged with it over endless plains for days on end, to the point of complete exhaustion. And yet both the Olympic runner and Makarios of Alexandria considered the reward so desirable that it outweighed all their travails. Do you know what it's like to hear the applause in an enormous Olympic amphitheater? There is no greater joy! Saint Makarios knew very well why he was carrying baskets of sand on his back. The fame of his record-breaking desert pilgrimages soon spread throughout the Christian world. And Saint Makarios was just like your Olympic runner: After winning the five-thousand-meter race came the ten-thousand-meter race, and after winning that he could not rest until he had triumphed in the marathon as well. The thirst for admiration is unquenchable. Saint Makarios arrived unrecognized at the Tabis monastery and asked to be accepted as an ordinary monk. He waited for the forty-day fast to begin, and then his moment of glory came: While all the others fasted sitting down, he remained standing throughout the forty-day period! You can't even imagine this kind of triumph! Or think of Saint Simeon Stylites. In the middle of the desert he built himself a pillar with a platform on top, just big enough to stand on. And he remained standing on top of this pillar for the rest of his life, while the Christian world enthusiastically admired his unbelievable record, an achievement whereby man seemed to transcend his human limitations. Saint Simeon was the Yuri Gagarin of the fifth century. Can you imagine the happiness that filled Saint Anne of Paris when she heard through a Gaulish trading mission that Saint Simeon knew about her life and blessed her from atop his pillar? And why do you think he was so eager to break the record? Was it because he had renounced his ties to life and to things of this world? Don't be naïve! The Church fathers realized perfectly well that Saint Simeon was full of vainglory, and they subjected him to a test. In the name of their spiritual authority they ordered him to come down from his pillar and to cease striving for a record. What a blow to Saint Simeon! But he was wise enough, or crafty enough, to obey. The Church fathers were not opposed to his activity, they only wanted to make sure that his vanity did not exceed his obedience. As soon as they saw him dejectedly descending from his perch, they ordered him to climb back up. So Saint Simeon remained on top of his pillar until his death, having earned the love and admiration of the world."

Olga listened attentively, but at Bartleff's last words she broke into laughter.

"That enormous thirst for admiration is not ridiculous but moving," said Bartleff. "A person who longs to be admired clings to people, feels closely tied to them, cannot live without them. Saint Simeon was alone in space, on a single square meter of pillar. Yet he was communing with all mankind! In his imagination he saw millions of eyes avidly fixed on him, and this gladdened his heart. It is a great example of love for mankind and love for life. You have no idea, dear Olga, what a strong influence Simeon Stylites exerts on us to this day. To this day, he is a living presence within us all."

There was a knock on the door, and in came the waiter pushing before him a cart laden with food. He spread a tablecloth and proceeded to set the table. Bartleff reached into the cigar box and dropped a handful of coins into the waiter's pocket. They all started eating, with the waiter standing at their backs, filling their glasses with wine and serving one course after another.

Bartleff appreciatively commented upon the various dishes, and Skreta remarked that he could not remember when he had eaten so well. "Perhaps the last time I enjoyed a meal so much was when my mother was still alive and cooked for me, but I was just a little boy then. I was orphaned at the age of five. The world into which I was thrown seemed strange, and its food tasted strange, too. Enjoyment of food can take place only in an atmosphere of love."

"That's quite true," agreed Bartleff, lifting a morsel of beef with his fork.

"A lonely child loses his appetite. To this day there is an ache inside me whenever I recall that I have neither mother nor father. I have knocked about in this world, but believe me, I'd still give my right arm to have a daddy."

"You overestimate family ties," said Bartleff. "All people are your near and dear ones. Don't forget what Jesus said when they tried to call him back to his mother and brothers. He pointed at his disciples and said: 'Here are my mother and my brothers.'"

Dr. Skreta countered: "All the same, the Church did not have the slightest intention of impairing family ties or replacing the family with some kind of loose communalism."

"The Church is not Jesus. And if you will permit me to say so, in my eyes Saint Paul was not only a disciple of Jesus but a falsifier of his teaching. His somersault from Saul to Paul—haven't we seen enough of those passionate fanatics who jump overnight from one faith to another? And let nobody tell me that fanatics are motivated by love! They are moralists mumbling their ten commandments. But Jesus was not a moralist. Just recall what he said when they reproached him for insufficient respect toward the Sabbath: 'The Sabbath was made for man, not man for the Sabbath.' Jesus loved women! Can you imagine Saint Paul as a lover? Saint Paul would condemn me because I love women. But not Jesus. I see nothing wrong in loving women, many women, and in being loved by them in return." Bartleff was smiling, pleased with himself. "Friends, I didn't have an easy life and I've been face to face with death several times. But in one respect God has been generous to me: I have known many women, and I have known their love."

The repast was finished and the waiter was already beginning to clear the table when there was another knock on the door. It was a weak, shy knock, as if someone were waiting for encouragement. Bartleff said: "Come in."

The door opened and in came a child, a little girl about five years old. The child was wearing a white dress with puffed sleeves and belted with a broad white ribbon which was tied in the back into a huge double bow resembling a pair of wings. She was holding a flower in her hand, a large dahlia. When she saw the roomful of people, all of whom had stopped and turned their eyes toward her, she stopped still and did not dare go further.

Bartleff rose and said, beaming: "Don't be afraid, my angel, come on in."

The child, as if cuddled by Bartleff's smile, ran toward him laughing, Bartleff accepted the flower and kissed the girl on the forehead.

Everyone observing this scene, including the waiter, was struck with wonder. The child with her twin white bows really did resemble a winged angel. And Bartleff, leaning forward and holding the dahlia stem in his hand, looked like one of the baroque statues of saints which adorn the squares of provincial towns.

He turned to his guests. "Dear friends, I felt happy in your company and I hope you enjoyed the evening as much as I did. I'd like to sit with you late into the night, but you can see that this is impossible. This lovely angel calls me to someone who is waiting. I told you that life has persecuted me in many ways, but I've been fortunate in the love of women."

Bartleff held the dahlia against his breast. His other hand was touching the little girl's shoulder, and he was bowing in all directions. To Olga he seemed ridiculously theatrical. She was glad that he was leaving and she would be alone with Jakub at last.

Bartleff turned and led the child toward the door. But before leaving the room he reached into the cigar box and filled his pocket with a brimming handful of silver coins.

11

As soon as the waiter had finished stacking the dishes and empty bottles on his cart and left the room, Olga said:

"Who was that little girl, anyway?"

"I never saw her before," replied Skreta.

"She really did look like a little angel," said Jakub.

Olga laughed. "An angel who procures mistresses?"

"Yes. A procurer and go-between. That's precisely what his personal angel should be like."

"I don't know whether she was an angel," said Skreta, "but it is certainly strange that I have never seen that child before, even though I know just about everybody in these parts."

"Then there is only one explanation," smiled Jakub. "She was not of this world."

"Whether she was an angel or the daughter of the local cleaning woman, there's one thing I'd bet on," said Olga. "There was no beloved woman waiting for him at all! He is an enormously self-centered person who can't stop bragging."

"I like him," said Jakub.

"All the same, I still say that he is the most self-centered human being on the face of this earth," retorted Olga. "I wouldn't be at all surprised if an hour before our visit he gave the little girl a handful of coins and asked her to show up here with a flower at such-and-such a time. Religious people have a great talent for staging miraculous scenes."

"I hope you are right," said Dr. Skreta. "You see, Mr. Bartleff is a very ill person, and every night of love involves great risks for him."

"There you are. I was right after all! All his hints about women were just so much empty talk!"

"My dear young lady," said Skreta, "I am his physician and his friend, and yet I am not sure about that. I simply don't know."

"Is his illness really serious?" asked Jakub.

"Why do you think he's been staying at this spa for more than a year now? His wife, whom he's crazy about, only comes up here every now and then."

"Without him it's rather gloomy here," said Jakub.

And in fact all three of them suddenly felt orphaned in the strange apartment and had no wish to stay longer.

Skreta rose from his chair. "I'll take Miss Olga home and then we can go for a little walk. We've still got a lot to talk about."

"I don't feel like going to sleep yet!" protested Olga.

"It's high time. As your doctor I order you to go to bed," Skreta said sternly.

They left Richmond House and set out across the park. Along the way Olga found an opportunity to whisper to Jakub: "I wanted to be alone with you tonight. . . ."

Jakub only shrugged his shoulders, for Skreta was imposing his will with great authority. They took the girl to the Marx House and in his friend's presence Jakub did not even kiss her on the cheek, as was his custom. The doctor's antipathy toward her prunelike bosom had unnerved him. He saw the disappointment in Olga's face and was sorry he had hurt her.

"So what do you say?" asked Skreta when he found himself alone with his friend. "You heard me explain that I needed a father.

A stone would have wept, but he just kept blathering about Saint Paul. Is it really so hard for him to get the point? For two years now I've been drumming it into his head that I am an orphan. I've been expounding on the advantages of an American passport. I must have told him a thousand anecdotes about various cases of adoption. I fully expected that he'd take the hint long ago and adopt me."

"He's too wrapped up in himself," said Jakub.

"That's it," Skreta agreed.

"You really can't blame him, if he's a sick man," retorted Jakub, adding: "Assuming, of course, that his condition is really as serious as you made out."

"It's even worse than that," said Skreta. "Six months ago he came down with a new infarct, a very severe one. Since that time he hasn't dared leave this place, and he lives here like a prisoner. His life hangs by a thread. And he knows it."

"In that case," said Jakub pensively, "you should have realized long ago that the indirect approach doesn't make sense, because your hints only dissolve in his own musings about himself. You should tell him what you want, quite directly and openly. I am sure he will agree, because he likes to please people. It fits in with his self-image. He wants to make people happy."

"You're a genius!" exclaimed Skreta, stopping in his tracks. "That's as simple as Columbus's egg, and you're absolutely right! Like an idiot I have wasted two years of my life just because I misjudged him! I lost two years through unnecessary hemming and hawing! And it's your fault because you should have advised me long ago!"

"You should have asked me!"

"You haven't come for a visit for over two years!"

The two friends walked briskly through the dark park, savoring the clear autumnal air.

"I've made him a father," said Skreta, "so it's only fair that he should make me a son!"

Jakub agreed.

"You know what my trouble is?" Skreta resumed after a long

pause. "I'm surrounded by idiots. Is there a single person in this place whom I can ask for advice? Intelligent people are born into a kind of absolute exile. I think about this night and day, because it's my field: humanity produces an incredible quantity of idiots. The dumber the individual, the greater his desire to multiply. The better individuals give birth to at most a single child, and the best—like yourself—come to the conclusion that they won't propagate at all. That's a catastrophe. I am always dreaming about a world where a man would be born not among strangers but among brothers."

Jakub listened to Skreta's arguments without finding them especially interesting. Skreta continued:

"I don't mean that as an empty phrase! I am not a politician but a doctor, and the word *brother* has a concrete meaning for me. Brothers are those who have at least one parent in common. All the sons of Solomon, even though they came from hundreds of different mothers, were brothers. That must have been beautiful! Don't you think so?"

Jakub breathed the cool night air and didn't know what to answer.

"Of course," Skreta continued, "it is very difficult to force people to govern their sex lives through considerations of their progeny. But that is not the crux of the matter, anyway. The twentieth century ought to be able to find new ways of solving the question of rational propagation of the human race. We can't go on mixing love and procreation forever."

With that idea Jakub found himself in agreement.

"You're only interested in liberating love from procreation," said Skreta. "But I am more interested in liberating procreation from love. I want to initiate you into my project. I have created a sperm bank using my own semen."

At last Jakub perked up his ears.

"What do you say to that?"

"It seems like an excellent idea."

"Isn't it? I have cured quite a few women of childlessness by using this approach. Don't forget that many wives are barren only because their husbands are sterile. I have a large clientele from all over the republic, and in addition, for the last four years I have been in charge of routine gynecologic examinations for this region. There is nothing easier than to pick up a syringe, fill it with the life-giving stuff, and inject it into these women."

"How many children have you got by now?"

"I've been doing this for several years, but I can only guess at the exact figures. Sometimes I can't be sure of my paternity, because my patients are unfaithful to me, so to speak, by sleeping with their husbands. Besides that, they go back to their own towns and often don't even let me know whether my treatment was successful. I have somewhat better control over my local patients."

Skreta paused, and Jakub gave himself over to tender musings. Skreta's project enraptured and moved him, for it was so characteristic of his old friend, the incorrigible dreamer. "It must be great to have so many children with so many women . . ." he said.

"And they're all brothers," added Skreta.

They strolled on, filling their lungs with the fragrant air. At last Skreta said:

"You know, I often tell myself that even though there are many things on this old planet of ours that we don't like, we can't get away from our responsibility. It makes me furious that I can't travel freely over the globe, but I would never permanently leave my homeland. And I'd never malign it. I'd have to malign myself first. What have any of us done to make our country better? What have we done to make it more livable? To turn it into a country where we'd really feel at home?" Skreta's voice turned soft, tender: "Home . . . a man can only feel at home among his own kind. Because you told me you're leaving, I decided that you've got to take part in my project. I have a test tube set aside for you. You'll be abroad, far away, yet in the meantime this land will give birth to your children! And in ten, twenty years you'll see what a lovely country this will turn into!"

A round moon hung in the sky (it will be there until the last night of our story, so that we can rightly call it a "Lunar Adventure"), and Dr. Skreta accompanied Jakub back to Richmond House. "Don't leave tomorrow," he said.

"I must. They are waiting for me," replied Jakub, but he knew that he could be swayed.

"Nonsense," said Skreta. "I am glad you like my plan. Tomorrow we'll discuss all its details."

Fourth
Day

1

As Mrs. Klima was leaving the house in the morning, her husband was still in bed.

"Isn't it time for you to get up?" she asked him.

"Why should I hurry? Those idiots don't deserve it," answered Klima, yawning and turning over.

He had already informed her that in the course of the tiresome conference a few days earlier he had been browbeaten into a pledge to donate some of his free time to amateur bands, and that on Thursday evening he was scheduled to take part in a concert in a certain mountain resort with a jazz-loving doctor and another amateur musician. He was cursing and fuming, but Mrs. Klima looked him in the face and knew perfectly well that all his anger was a sham and the whole story about a concert was only a trick to conceal some amorous intrigue. His face was an open book to her; he could never keep anything secret. Thus, as he now turned, muttering, to lie on his other side, she understood at once that he did not do so out of sleepiness but in order to hide his face and so prevent her from scrutinizing it.

Then she left for work. When illness had robbed her of her place in front of the footlights, he had found a job for her at the theater as a secretary. It was not a bad job, she was always meeting interesting people, and she enjoyed considerable freedom in arranging her work schedule.

She arrived at her office, sat down at her desk to draft several official letters, but found it difficult to concentrate.

Nothing can take possession of a person so completely as jealousy. Kamila's loss of her mother a year before was certainly a greater misfortune than one of the trumpeter's flirtations. And yet this bereavement hurt less, even though Kamila had been extremely fond of her mother. The pain of her loss was mercifully many-faceted: there was sorrow, longing, poignancy, self-reproach, even a quiet smile. And that pain was mercifully dispersed: from her mother's coffin her thoughts strayed back to her childhood, even further back into her mother's childhood; her thoughts busied themselves with dozens of practical tasks, with the wide-open future and with the faithful, consoling husband at her side (yes, during those exceptional days Klima was her consolation).

In contrast, the pain of jealousy was not diffused; it revolved like a drill around a single point. Her mother's death had opened a door to the future (a different, orphaned but more mature future); the pain of her husband's infidelity opened no door at all. Everything focused upon a single (ever-present) image of his unfaithful body, upon a single (ever-present) reproach. After her mother died Kamila had been able to listen to music, even to read; but during a bout of jealousy she was unable to do anything at all.

As soon as Klima mentioned his trip the idea occurred to her to go to the spa and check on the suspicious concert, but she rejected this plan because she knew how much Klima detested any manifestation of jealousy. But jealousy whirled inside her like a racing motor and she could not help lifting the telephone receiver. She pretended to herself that she was calling the railroad station without any specific intent, out of nervousness, out of sheer inability to concentrate on her correspondence.

She learned that the train was leaving at eleven o'clock in the morning. She saw herself trudging the sidewalks of an unfamiliar town, searching for a poster with Klima's name, inquiring in the spa office whether they knew of any concert to be given by her husband, finding out that no such concert was scheduled, and at last straggling, weary and betrayed, back home. She further imagined Klima telling her about the concert the next day, while she pressed him for details. She would look into his face, listen to his fictitious stories, and with bitter delight drink the poisonous brew of his lies.

She reprimanded herself at once, however: This was no way for her to act; she must not spend days and weeks on end in spying and jealous fantasizing. She was afraid of losing him—and in the end this very fear would drive him away from her!

But another voice answered with sly naïveté: After all, it was not a question of spying on him! Klima said that he was giving a concert, and she believed him completely! Precisely because she was putting all jealousy aside she was accepting his statement at face value, without the slightest suspicion! Hadn't he said that he was reluctant to go, dreaded having to spend a boring day and night there? That is why she wanted to follow him, to spring a happy surprise! At the end of the concert a disgruntled Klima would be taking his bows, thinking of the long, tiresome trip home—and presto! She'd suddenly appear at the foot of the stage, he'd see her with happy surprise, and they would enjoy a good laugh together!

She stepped into the director's office and handed him her carefully drafted letters. They liked her at the theater; she was the wife of a famous musician, and yet she was unassuming and friendly. Everyone was disarmed by the air of sadness that often emanated from her, and the director generally bent over backward to be nice to her. Now, he readily agreed to her request for some time off. She promised to be back Friday afternoon, and to stay late that day until all the work was finished.

2

It was ten o'clock and Olga followed her usual routine. She received from Ruzena a large white sheet and a key, then went to her cabana, undressed, hung her clothes on a hanger, wrapped the sheet around herself like a toga, locked the cabin, returned the key to Ruzena, and went to the adjoining hall where the pool was. She threw the sheet over the railing and climbed down the metal ladder to join a number of other women who were already immersed in the water. The pool was not big, but Olga was convinced that swimming was important to her health so she attempted a few strokes. This produced a wave which splashed water into the talking mouth of one of the ladies. "What's the matter with you?" she shouted at Olga testily. "This is not a swimming pool!"

Women were sitting around the edge of the basin like huge frogs. Olga was afraid of them. All of them were older than she, they were bigger, had more fat and skin. She sat down humbly among them, hunched into herself and frowning.

Then she suddenly noticed that there was someone standing by the door, a young man of short stature, dressed in blue jeans and a tattered sweater.

"What's that young man doing here?" she exclaimed.

All the women turned in the direction Olga was pointing and began to laugh and giggle. Ruzena appeared and announced loudly: "The film people have arrived. They are going to shoot a newsreel of everybody."

The women broke into a new wave of laughter.

"What a silly idea!" protested Olga.

"They have official permission," said Ruzena.

"I don't care. Nobody asked me for my permission!" protested Olga angrily.

The young man in the torn sweater, a light meter dangling from his neck, stepped closer to the pool and gazed at Olga with a smile which she found insolent. "Miss, thousands of people will go out of their minds when they see you on the screen!"

The women responded with a new burst of laughter. Olga covered her breasts with her hands (that was not difficult, for as we know they resembled a pair of prunes) and crouched behind the others.

Two more men in jeans walked in, and the taller one said: "Please, ladies, act quite natural, as if we weren't here at all."

Olga reached for the sheet draped over the railing, quickly wrapped herself up in it, and climbed out to the tiled edge of the pool. The sheet was dripping wet.

"Oh shit! Where the hell are you going?" the youth in the tattered sweater shouted at her.

"You're scheduled for another fifteen minutes in the pool!" Ruzena called to her.

"She's shy!" they laughed behind her back.

"She's afraid someone might spoil that perfect beauty of hers," said Ruzena.

"A princess!" chimed in a voice from the pool.

"Anybody who does not want to be in the picture is of course free to leave," said the tall man calmly.

"We've nothing to be ashamed of! We're all mermaids!" a fat lady said in a resounding voice, and the surface of the water shook with laughter.

"But that girl had no right to leave! She's supposed to stay here another fifteen minutes!" protested Ruzena as Olga strode defiantly to her cabana.

3

Nobody could blame Ruzena for being in a bad mood. But why was she so irritated by Olga's refusal to let herself be filmed? Why did she identify so completely with the collective of plump matrons who greeted the arrival of the men with squeals and giggles? And why were those women squealing with joy, anyway? Surely not because they wanted to impress the young men with their charms and to seduce them?

No. But their show of impudence stemmed from the knowledge that they had no seductive charms at their disposal. They were full of distaste for youthful feminine loveliness and longed to exhibit their sexually useless bodies as a mocking insult to naked femininity. They yearned to torpedo the glory of feminine beauty, for they knew that in the last analysis one body is more or less like another, and ugliness revenges itself against beauty by whispering in a man's ear: Look, this is the real truth of that feminine figure you find so bewitching! Look, this repellent, sagging mammary gland is the same thing as that shapely breast you so foolishly adore!

The mirthful ribaldry of the matrons in the pool was a necrophiliac victory celebration over the transience of youth and it was made all the more jubilant by the presence of a sacrificial young girl. When Olga covered herself in a sheet they perceived this as an act of defiance of their wicked ceremony, and they became furious.

But what about Ruzena? She was neither fat nor old, in fact she was prettier than Olga. Why then did she feel no sense of solidarity with her?

Had she been determined to get rid of her baby and confident of a happy life with Klima, she would have reacted quite differently. A man's love lifts a woman out of the crowd and Ruzena would have blissfully savored her uniqueness. In the fat matrons she would have seen her enemies and in Olga her sister. She would have wished her well, as beauty smiles on beauty, happiness on happiness, love on love.

But the previous night Ruzena had slept very poorly and had come to the decision that she could not put her trust in Klima's love; thus, everything which had promised to lift her out of the crowd now appeared to be delusion. All she had was that tiny bud sprouting in her belly, protected by society and tradition. All she had was the glorious communality of the female lot, a communality that promised to come to her defense.

Those women in the pool were an incarnation of universal femaleness: the femaleness of eternal childbearing, nursing, flowering, and wilting, the femaleness that laughs at that fleeting second when a woman believes she is loved and when she feels herself to be unique.

There is no possible compromise between the woman who believes in her uniqueness and her sisters enveloped in the mantle of common femaleness. After a sleepless, brain-racking night, Ruzena firmly placed herself (alas, poor trumpeter) on the side of ageless, universal womanhood.

4

Jakub was driving, with Bobis sitting at his side and every now and then attempting to lick his face. Beyond the last houses of the town loomed several high-rise buildings. These apartment houses had sprung up since the year before and to Jakub they seemed horrible. They stuck out of the green landscape like brooms in a flowerbed. Jakub patted the dog on the head, and the dog continued to gaze placidly at the countryside. It occurred to Jakub that it was merciful of God not to have burdened the small brains of dogs with an aesthetic sense.

The dog once more licked the side of Jakub's face (perhaps sensing that he was on Jakub's mind), and Jakub told himself that his country was getting neither better nor worse but only more and more absurd. He had once lived through a hunt for human beings and yesterday he witnessed a hunt for dogs, and had the impression of seeing the same play with different casts of characters. The roles of policemen were taken by aging pensioners and the roles of political prisoners by a bulldog, a nondescript mutt, and a dachshund.

He recalled that several years earlier his neighbors in the capital had found their cat in front of their door with his tongue cut out, his legs tied, and nails hammered into both eye sockets. Neighborhood children were playing grown-up games. Jakub stroked Bobis on the head and parked in front of the inn.

As he stepped out of the car he assumed that the dog would at once happily streak for the door of his home. Instead, Bobis jumped all over Jakub and wanted to play. But there was a loud call, "Bobis!" and the dog ran toward a woman standing in the doorway.

"You're a hopeless philanderer," she said to the dog, and asked Jakub apologetically whether the dog had been annoying him.

When he explained that he had spent the night with the

animal and driven out this morning just to return him to his owners, the woman thanked him profusely and cordially invited him to come into the house. She asked him to make himself comfortable in a special room apparently used for private banquets, and scurried off to fetch her husband.

A while later she returned with a young man who pulled up a chair alongside Jakub and shook his hand. "You must be a very kindhearted man to come all the way out here just on account of Bobis. He is a real tramp, he's always roaming around. But we're fond of him. Would you care for some lunch?"

"Yes, thank you," said Jakub, and the woman hurried off to the kitchen. Jakub recounted how he had saved Bobis from a squad of pole-carrying pensioners.

"The bastards!" exclaimed the young man, and called out to his wife: "Vera! Come here! I want you to hear the latest about those bastards down there in the town!"

Vera returned carrying a tray with a steaming tureen. She pulled up a chair and Jakub had to narrate once more the story of yesterday's events. The dog sat under the table, letting himself be scratched behind the ears.

After Jakub had finished the soup, the man got up and brought a dish of roast pork and dumplings from the kitchen.

Jakub sat by the window. He felt content. The man was cursing the bastards "down there in the town" (it fascinated Jakub that the man considered his inn to be an elevated place, a detached Olympus, a lofty observatory). His wife led in a two-year-old boy: "Say thank you to this gentleman. He brought you back your Bobis."

The child babbled a few unintelligible words and grinned at Jakub. The sun was shining and yellowing leaves fluttered gently on the ground outside the window. Everything was calm; the inn was high above the tumult of the world and was filled with peace.

Even though he had no desire for progeny, Jakub liked children. "You have a nice little boy," he said.

"He's a queer duck," replied the woman. "God knows where he got that banana of a nose."

Jakub at once thought of his friend. He said: "Dr. Skreta told me that you were a patient of his."

"You know the doctor?" the young man asked eagerly.

"He's an old chum of mine."

"We are very grateful to him," remarked the young mother, and Jakub told himself that this child might well represent one of the successes of Skreta's eugenics project.

"He's not a doctor, he's a magician!" the young man said with reverence.

It occurred to Jakub that in the peaceful, Bethlehem-like environment the couple and their child seemed like a holy family and that their son did not descend from a human father but from a divine physician.

The big-nosed child gurgled some more words and the young man gazed at him lovingly. Then he turned to his wife. "Who knows? Maybe one of your distant ancestors sported a long schnozzle."

Jakub laughed, for a peculiar question sprang to his mind: Did Skreta's own wife, Kvcta, owe her pregnancy to a glass syringe?

"Isn't that possible?" laughed the youthful father.

"You're right," Jakub replied. "It is a great consolation to think that we might long be dead and buried while our nose still continues to roam the earth."

They all had a good laugh, and the idea in Jakub's mind that Skreta might be the little boy's father slowly dissolved into a mere fanciful dream.

5

Franta took the money from the lady whose refrigerator he had just fixed. He walked out of the house, mounted his faithful motorcycle, and drove to the edge of town to turn the day's accounts over to the office in charge of maintenance services for the district.

By two o'clock he was through for the day. He started up his motorcycle again and drove to the spa. In the parking lot he saw a white roadster. He parked the cycle alongside it and walked down the colonnade to the social hall, because he suspected that the trumpeter might be there.

He was driven neither by arrogance nor belligerence. He had no desire to create a scene. On the contrary, he was determined to suppress his feelings, to humble himself, to submit. He told himself that his love was so great that he was ready to suffer anything for its sake. Just as a fairy-tale prince bears all kinds of hardships and suffering for the sake of his princess, fighting dragons and swimming oceans, so he, too, was ready to undergo heroic trials.

Why was he so humble? Why instead did he not look around for other girls, present at the spa in such alluring abundance?

Franta was younger than Ruzena, and it was his misfortune to suffer from the inexperience of youth. When he grows up he will become aware of the transitory nature of the world and he will learn that no sooner does one woman disappear from the horizon than a galaxy of other women comes into view. But Franta still knows nothing about time. Ever since childhood he has been living in an unchanging world, in a kind of fixed eternity; he still has the same father and mother, and Ruzena, who made him into a man, arches over him like the vault of the sky, the only sky there is. He cannot imagine life without her.

He had obediently promised to stop spying on her, and he was sincerely determined to stay out of her way. He told himself that he was interested only in the trumpeter, and tracking him would not actually be a breach of his promise. At the same time he realized, of course, that this was only an excuse and that Ruzena would be sure to condemn his behavior, but there was something driving him which was stronger than any reflection or resolution, something as strong as a craving for drugs: he had to see the man, had to look at him again, slowly and close up. He had to look into his tormentor's face. He had to look at his body, because its union with the body of Ruzena seemed unimaginable and incredible. He had to look, as if his eyes could tell him whether their bodies were indeed capable of uniting.

A rehearsal was in progress. On stage were Dr. Skreta at the drums, some short fellow at the piano, and Klima with his trumpet. In the hall sat a handful of young men, jazz fans who had wandered in to listen. Franta had no fear that the reason for his presence would be detected. He was certain that the trumpeter, blinded by the light of the motorcycle, had not seen his face on Tuesday, and thanks to Ruzena's reticence nobody else knew much about his relationship with her.

The trumpeter interrupted the music and sat down at the piano to demonstrate to the short fellow the right tempo for a certain passage. Franta sat on a chair in the back, slowly turning into a shadow which would not leave the trumpeter for a single moment that day.

6

He was driving back from the inn, sorry that there was no longer a cheerful dog by his side to lick his face. It occurred to him what a miracle it was that for forty-five years of his life he had managed to keep the seat by his side empty, so that he could now leave the country so easily, without baggage, without burdens, alone, with a deceptive (and yet beautiful) sense of youthfulness, like a student just beginning to lay the foundation of his career.

He tried to absorb fully the idea that he was on the point of leaving his homeland. He tried to recall his past life, to envision it as a broad landscape he was regretfully leaving behind, an immense landscape stretching to the horizon. But he found it hard to do so. What he did manage to see in his imagination was small, limited, flattened, like a closed accordion. Only with great effort was he able to summon up a few memories capable of coalescing into a semblance of a grand, destiny-filled life.

He looked at the trees lining the road. Their leaves were green, red, yellow, brown. The forest resembled a conflagration. He was pleased to think that he was leaving at a time when the woods were burning and his life and memories were being consumed in those beautiful, heartless flames. Why should he feel sorry about not feeling sorrow? Regret feeling no regret?

No, he was not sorry to leave, but neither did he feel any need to rush his departure. According to the plans he had made with friends abroad, he should already have crossed the border, but he realized that he was once more falling prey to that habit of procrastination for which he was notorious and for which his friends often jokingly took him to task. He always seemed to succumb to this mood precisely at those moments that called for definite, decisive action. He knew that he would proclaim all day long his pressing need for immediate departure, yet he also knew that since morning he had been doing everything in his power to prolong his stay in the pleasant resort, a place he had been visiting for years—sometimes after long intervals, but always with the happy anticipation of seeing his old friend.

He parked his car (yes, the trumpeter's white roadster and Franta's red motorcycle were already standing in the same lot) and he walked into the restaurant where he was shortly to meet Olga. He would have liked the table in back near the window looking out on the park with its colorful foliage, but unfortunately a man was just sitting down there. Jakub took a seat nearby. He could not see the park from there, but he was intrigued by the man who had taken the window table: he appeared markedly nervous, continually tapping his foot while keeping his eyes fixed on the entrance of the restaurant.

7

She arrived at last. Klima jumped up, rushed toward her, and led her to the window table. He was smiling at her, and that smile was trying to say "our understanding still stands, we trust each other, we're calm and confident, everything's fine." He searched the girl's face for an affirmative response but failed to find it. That made him uneasy. He was afraid to talk about the subject that was disquieting to him, and instead launched into meaningless small talk intended to create a lighthearted atmosphere. However, his words rebounded against her silence as if they had struck a cliff.

Suddenly she interrupted: "I've changed my mind. It would be a crime. You may be capable of doing something like that. But not me."

Inside the trumpeter, everything crumbled. He looked numbly at Ruzena and found nothing to say. He felt only hopeless exhaustion. And Ruzena repeated: "It would be a crime."

He looked at her. She seemed unreal. This woman, whose likeness he had not been able to call to mind, now appeared before him as a lifelong sentence of doom. (Like all of us, Klima regarded as real only what enters consciousness from the inside, gradually, organically, whereas what comes from outside, unexpectedly and accidentally, he perceived as an invasion of unreality. Unfortunately, nothing is more real than such unreality.)

Then the waiter appeared, the same one who had recognized the trumpeter two days earlier. He was bringing a tray with two glasses of brandy, and said jovially: "I hope I am anticipating your wishes." Turning to Ruzena, he made the same remark as the last time: "Watch out! The girls will scratch your eyes out!" And he guffawed.

Klima was so caught up in his terror that he did not grasp the waiter's words. He took a gulp of cognac and leaned toward

Ruzena. "What's gotten into you? I thought we had everything straightened out. I thought we understood each other. Why did you change your mind all of a sudden? You agreed that we first needed a couple of years all to ourselves. Please, Ruzena! We love each other! Let's not have a baby until we both really want it!"

8

Jakub at once recognized the girl as the nurse who had wanted to turn Bobis over to the old men. He watched her intently, eager to know what she and the man were talking about. He could not make out a single word, but he sensed that the conversation was full of tension.

It soon became obvious from the man's face that he had learned some depressing news. It took him a while before he was able to recover. His expression showed that he was pleading with the girl. But she remained resolutely silent.

Jakub had the impression that someone's life was at stake. He still regarded the blonde as the bystander obligingly helping to pin down a victim for the executioner, and he did not doubt for one moment that the young man was on the side of life and that she was on the side of death. The young man was trying to save a life, he was begging for help, but the girl was refusing and because of her someone would die.

And then he saw the man stop pleading, smile and even stroke the girl's cheek. Had they reached an agreement? Not at all. The eyes under the blond hair were relentlessly staring into the distance, avoiding the man's face.

Jakub could not tear his eyes away from the young woman, a woman he could no longer see in any way except as a hangman's helper. Her face was pretty but empty. Pretty to attract a man, empty to make the man's pitiful pleas vanish without a trace. That face was proud, too, and it occurred to Jakub that it was not proud of its prettiness but precisely of its vacuity.

It seemed to Jakub that this face stood for thousands of others he had known. His whole life seemed to be an endless dialogue with this face. Whenever he had tried to explain, that face had haughtily turned aside. It had defeated his arguments by switching to other subjects, it had mocked his smiles by calling him flippant, it had denied his requests by accusing him of arrogance—that face that understood nothing and decided everything, a face as barren as a desert and proud of its barrenness.

It occurred to him that he was setting eyes on it for the last time, and that tomorrow he would leave its realm forever.

9

Ruzena noticed Jakub, too, and recognized him. She was aware of his fixed gaze and it made her nervous. It seemed to her that she was surrounded by two secretly allied men, two stares aimed at her head like two pairs of gun barrels.

Klima was repeating his arguments and she was at a loss how to answer. She tried to reassure herself that when a baby's life hung in the balance, logic was beside the point and only feelings mattered. She turned away from both gazes and looked out the window.

In the course of this inward concentration, a vague sense of her identity as betrayed, beloved, and misunderstood mother was beginning to stir in her, and a feeling of outrage was rising in her soul like yeasty dough. Since she was unable to express it in words, she let it speak through her eyes, which were stubbornly staring at a spot in the adjoining park.

But precisely at that spot where her unflinching gaze was focused she suddenly saw a familiar figure. She was so startled that she no longer heard what Klima was saying to her. This was the third set of eyes pointing straight at her like the barrels of a gun, and this gun was the most dangerous of all. At the beginning (that is to say, a few weeks back) Ruzena still had not reached certainty as to who had actually caused her impending motherhood. The young man, now trying to spy on her, half hidden behind a park tree, had to be taken into consideration as one of the possibilities. But that was only at the beginning, for as time went on she began to lean more and more toward the trumpeter as her true impregnator, until she finally decided that he must surely have been the one. Let us be quite clear on this point: she had no intention of pinning paternity on him deceitfully. She chose not deceit but truth: she simply decided that this was how it must *truly* have happened.

Besides, she found it impossible to believe that an occurrence as sacred as maternity might have been brought about by someone whom she virtually despised. It was not a question of logic; she had simply convinced herself by a kind of suprarational illumination that she could have become pregnant only by someone whom she liked, respected, and admired. And when she heard over the telephone that he whom she had chosen as the father of her child was shocked and resentful of his paternal mission, the die was cast; at that instant she not only became completely certain that she had chosen truth, but she was ready to fight for it.

Klima lapsed into silence and stroked Ruzena's cheek. Startled out of her musing, she noticed that he was smiling. He said that they should take another ride into the country, for this table was separating them like a wall.

She was afraid. Franta was still crouched behind the tree, looking into the restaurant window. What if he were to bother them again as soon as they stepped outside? What if he were to make another scene, as he had done on Tuesday?

"Check, please. We had two brandies," Klima was just saying to the waiter.

She pulled a glass tube out of her purse.

The trumpeter handed the waiter a banknote and with a sweeping gesture refused the change.

Ruzena opened the tube, shook out a pill, and quickly swallowed it. By the time she was about to twist the top of the tube closed the trumpeter had turned to her again and looked at her imploringly. He reached out for her hands, their fingers touched, and she let the tube drop onto the tablecloth. "Come, let's go," he said, and Ruzena got up. She saw Jakub's stare, intense and unfriendly, and she quickly shifted her eyes.

As they reached the street, she looked anxiously toward the park but Franta was no longer there.

10

Jakub rose, picked up his half-empty glass of wine, and moved to the vacated table. With satisfaction he looked out the window at the reddening trees in the park, and told himself once more that this was a pyre onto which he was casting forty-five years of life on this planet. Then his glance happened to move down toward the tabletop, and he noticed the glass tube lying next to the ashtray. He picked it up and examined it. The label bore the name of a drug which was unfamiliar to him, and a penciled reminder: *3 × daily*. The tablets inside the tube were of a pale blue color. That seemed remarkable.

These were the last hours of life in his homeland, the smallest events took on extraordinary significance and were transformed into allegorical drama. What does it mean, he asked himself, that this day of all days someone left me a tube of pale blue pills? And why was this tube bequeathed to me by a very particular kind of woman— persecutor's handmaiden, executioner's friend? Was she trying to tell me that the need for pale blue pills has not yet passed? Or was she reminding me of poison in order to affirm her undying hatred? Or was she trying to let me know that my departure from this country is an act of capitulation, equivalent to swallowing the pale blue pill I carry in my vest pocket?

He reached into his pocket, pulled out the tiny package, and unwrapped it. Now that he was actually seeing his pill, it seemed to be a somewhat darker shade of blue than the medication in the tube. He opened the tube and shook out one of the pills. Yes, his was definitely a trace darker and a bit smaller. He dropped both pills into the tube. Now they looked so similar that a quick glance would not show the difference. The topmost of the pills, probably intended for a trivial medicinal purpose, now couched death.

At that moment Olga appeared. He quickly closed the lid, put the tube down on the table next to the ashtray, and rose to greet his friend.

"I thought I just recognized the trumpeter Klima. Is that possible?" she said breathlessly, sitting down across the table from Jakub. "He was arm in arm with that awful woman! You've no idea what a time I had with her today in the pool—"

She stopped short because at that moment Ruzena appeared at their table and said: "I left my medicine here."

Before Jakub could answer, she saw the tube lying near the ashtray and reached out for it.

But Jakub beat her to it.

"Give it to me!" said Ruzena.

"I want to ask you a favor," said Jakub. "Could you let me have one of those pills?"

"Please, stop it, I haven't got time. . . ."

"I am taking exactly the same kind of medicine and . . ."

"I am not a mobile pharmacy," said Ruzena.

Jakub was about to open the lid of the tube, but before he was able to do so Ruzena grabbed for it. Jakub quickly grasped the tube in his fist and pulled his hand out of the girl's reach.

"What are you doing? Give me those pills!" she shouted at him.

Jakub stared into her eyes, and then slowly, ceremoniously, he opened his hand.

11

The rhythmic clatter of the wheels seemed to be pounding a message of the utter futility of her trip. After all, she was quite sure her husband was not at the spa. Then why bother going there? Was she taking a four-hour train ride just to find out what she already knew, turn around, and ride home again? She was not driven by reason but by some engine that kept spinning faster and faster and could not be stopped. (At this point, both Kamila and Franta sweep into our story like two rockets steered by blind jealousy—if that can be called "steering.")

The rail connections between the capital and the mountain resort were not very good, and Mrs. Klima had to change trains three times. She was quite tired when she at last emerged on the picturesque platform, full of posters advertising the healing powers of local springs and mudbaths. She walked down the poplar-lined lane to the spa, and as she reached the colonnade her eye was caught by a hand-painted poster with her husband's name prominently spelled out in red letters. She stopped, greatly surprised, and under her husband's name read two other masculine names. She couldn't believe it: Klima had told the truth! It was just as he had said. In the first few seconds she felt an enormous joy, the return of a long-lost sense of trust.

But her joy was short-lived, for she soon came to the realization that the mere existence of a concert in no way proved her husband's fidelity. He might have agreed to perform in this remote spa only because it gave him a good opportunity to meet one of his mistresses. She suddenly became aware that everything was actually far worse than she had feared, and that she was trapped.

She had come to the spa in order to prove that her husband was not there, and thus to convict him *indirectly* of deceiving her (as she had so many, many times before). But now the situation was different: she was not about to convict him of a lie, but to catch him (*directly*, visibly) in an act of infidelity. Whether she wanted to or not, she was about to set eyes on the woman with whom Klima was spending the day. This idea almost made her knees shake. True, she had long been certain that she *knew* all there was to know, but until now she had never *seen* anything (any of his women). To be perfectly honest, she actually knew very little, she was only under the impression that she knew and gave this impression the weight of certainty. Her faith in his unfaithfulness was like a Christian's belief in the existence of God. The Christian believes in God in the full certainty that He will remain invisible. The idea that this day she would see Klima with a strange woman filled her with the kind of terror a Christian might feel on receiving a telephone call from God, announcing that He was coming over for dinner.

Anxiety gripped her whole body. Then she heard someone calling her name. She turned around and saw three young men standing in the middle of the colonnade. They wore sweaters and blue jeans, and their bohemian flair distinguished them unmistakably from the boringly meticulous looks of the other guests strolling by. They smiled at her.

"Salud!" she called out to them. They were film people, friends from her days on the stage.

The tallest one, a director, took her by the arm. "How marvelous it would be to imagine that you came on our account, just to see us. . . ."

"Instead, she came to see a mere husband," his assistant said mournfully.

"What bad luck," said the director. "The most beautiful woman in the whole capital, and one trumpeter manages to keep her all for himself, locked up in a cage for years on end. . . ."

"Shit!" said the cameraman (the youth in the torn sweater). "Let's go and celebrate!"

They thought they were offering admiration to a radiant queen who took an indifferent glance at their tribute before throwing it into a chest already brimming with other disdained gifts.

Instead, she was clutching their compliments like a lame girl grateful for an arm to lean on.

12

Olga kept on chattering while Jakub's mind was occupied by the thought that he had just given poison to a stranger, who might swallow it at any moment.

It had happened so suddenly, faster than he had been able to grasp. It had happened without his awareness.

Olga was bitterly recounting her recent experiences and Jakub mentally tried to convince himself that he had not really wanted to give the tube to the girl, but that she herself had forced him to do it.

The instant this thought occurred to him he realized that it was a cheap excuse. He could have availed himself of a thousand possibilities for refusing the girl's request. To her arrogance he could have opposed his own arrogance, while calmly removing the uppermost tablet and sticking it in his pocket.

And although he had lacked the presence of mind to do that, he could still have run after her and confessed that the tube contained poison. After all, it would not have been too difficult to explain how the whole thing had come about.

Yet here he was, sitting at a table and listening to Olga when he should be running after that nurse. There still was time. And it was his duty to do everything he could to save her life. Why then was he sitting still?

Olga talked on and he wondered why he kept sitting.

He decided that he must get up at once and look for the nurse. He tried to think of a way of explaining to Olga that he must leave her at once. Should he confide the whole story to her? He realized that he must not do that. What if the nurse swallowed the pill before he had a chance to stop her? Could he allow Olga to know that he was a murderer? And even if he got to the nurse in time, how could he justify to Olga the long hesitation before he had acted? How could he explain why he had allowed the woman to take the tube at all? The past few minutes of vacillation would already suffice to convict him of murder in the eyes of any observer!

No, he certainly could not confess to Olga, but what should he say to her? How could he justify suddenly jumping up from the table and running off somewhere?

But then, what difference would it make what he said to her? Why was he occupying himself with such nonsense? A life was at stake; what did it matter what Olga thought?

He knew that his cogitations were totally irrelevant and that every second of hesitation increased the nurse's danger. Actually, it was too late already. During the time he had been procrastinating, she and her companion had already gotten so far from the restaurant that he wouldn't even know where to look for them. How could he guess where they had gone? In what direction?

Yet he realized perfectly well that this, too, was just another excuse. It would be difficult to find them quickly, but not impossible. It was not too late to do something, but he must do something at once, before it was too late!

"It's been a bad day for me from the moment I got up," Olga was saying. "I overslept, I was late for breakfast, and they didn't want to serve me anymore, the pool was full of those stupid film people. And I was so anxious for this day to be perfect, because it's our last day together. You don't know how much that means to me. Jakub, do you have any idea how much it means to me?"

She leaned over the table and grasped his hands.

"Don't worry, everything will turn out fine," he said with great effort, unable to concentrate on Olga. A voice was constantly reminding him that the nurse had poison in her handbag and that he was responsible for her life or death. This voice was obtrusively incessant and yet at the same time remarkably weak, as if coming from abysmal depths.

13

Klima was driving down a forest road, and he came to the conclusion that this time treating Ruzena to a ride in his luxurious car was not going to produce any beneficial results. Ruzena refused to let herself be cajoled out of her stubborn aloofness, and the trumpeter lapsed into prolonged silence. At last, when the silence had become too oppressive, he said:

"You're coming to the concert, aren't you?"

"I don't know," she answered.

"Please come," he said, and the upcoming event served as a pretext for conversation which momentarily let them forget their quarrel. Klima tried to present an amusing portrait of the drum playing doctor, and he decided to postpone the crucial showdown with Ruzena until evening.

"I look forward to seeing you after the concert," he said. "It will be like the last time I played here. . . ." As soon as the words were out of his mouth he realized their significance. *Like the last time* meant that after the concert they would make love to each other. Good Lord, how had he completely failed to consider this possibility?

It was odd, but until that moment the idea that he might sleep with her again had not occurred to him at all. Her pregnancy had transformed her, quietly and unobtrusively, into a being associated not with sex but with trouble and anxiety. True, he had told himself that he should be loving toward her, that he should kiss and pet her, and he conscientiously tried to, but only as a gesture without any physical significance.

When he thought about it he recognized that his lack of interest in Ruzena's body was the greatest oversight he had made in the past few days. Yes, it was all perfectly clear now (and he was angry at friends he had consulted for not having called it to his attention): it was absolutely essential that he sleep with her! No doubt that aloof mood which the girl had so unexpectedly assumed and which proved so difficult for him to penetrate had been brought on precisely by the continuing separation of their bodies. His rejection of the baby—the flower of her womb—was a rejection of her pregnant body. This was all the more reason for him to show an interest in her physicality, to play off her girlish body against her maternal body and make it his ally.

After completing this analysis he felt new hope stirring within him. He squeezed Ruzena's shoulder and leaned closer. "I hate to have us quarrel. Let's not worry, everything will turn out all right. The main thing is that we're together. Let's save this night for ourselves, and it will be just as beautiful a night as our last one."

He was holding the wheel with one arm and the other was around her shoulders. Somewhere deep down there stirred a longing for her bare skin, and this gave him joy, for physical desire might prove to be a common language with which he could reach her at last.

"And where will I meet you?" she asked.

Klima realized that meeting her after the concert invited public recognition of their intimacy, but this could not be helped. "As soon as it's over, meet me backstage."

14

When Klima rushed off to the social hall for one last rehearsal, Ruzena took a long, searching look around. A while ago in the car she had spotted Franta in the rear-view mirror, following them on his motorcycle. But now he was nowhere in sight.

She felt like a fugitive from time. She knew that by tomorrow she would have to make up her mind what she wanted, and was as confused as ever. In the whole world there was not a single soul she trusted. Her own family seemed like strangers. Franta loved her, but for that very reason she mistrusted him (as the doe mistrusts the hunter). She mistrusted Klima (as the hunter mistrusts the doe). She was friendly with her colleagues, but she did not completely trust even them (as one hunter mistrusts another). She walked through life all alone, except that for the past few weeks she had been traveling with a strange companion inside her body, described by some as her greatest blessing and by others as the very opposite, a companion with whom she felt no real affinity at all.

She did not know. She was filled with unknowing. She did not even know where her feet were taking her.

She walked past the restaurant Slavia, the worst eating place in town, a dirty tavern where local citizens came to guzzle beer and to spit on the floor. It may have known better days, and from that period there remained a small garden with three wooden tables and chairs (once painted red but now faded and peeling), a memento of bourgeois delights—garden parties, outdoor dances, ladies' parasols coquettishly propped against a tree. But what did Ruzena know about those times, a girl who walked through life over a narrow bridge of the eternal present, a girl with no historical memory whatsoever! She failed to see the shadow of a long-vanished pink parasol, she only saw three men in blue jeans, one beautiful woman, and a bottle of wine standing on a bare table.

One of the men called out to her. She turned and recognized the cameraman in the torn sweater.

"Come and join us." He waved.

She complied.

"This lovely girl helped us shoot a short pornographic film today." The cameraman introduced Ruzena to a woman who reached out her hand and mumbled a name.

Ruzena sat down next to the cameraman. He put a glass in front of her and filled it with wine.

Ruzena was grateful that something was happening, that she didn't have to think about where to go and what to do, that she didn't have to decide about her baby.

15

At long last he finally reached some sort of decision. He paid the waiter and told Olga he had to leave her for a while and they would meet before the concert. Olga asked what it was he had to do, and Jakub had the unpleasant feeling of being interrogated. He answered that he must see Skreta.

"That's fine," she said. "I'm sure it won't take you very long. In the meantime I'll go and change, and I'll wait for you here at six. I'm inviting you to dinner."

Jakub accompanied Olga to Marx House. As soon as she disappeared down the hall, he turned to the doorman. "Tell me, do you know whether nurse Ruzena is in?"

"No, she isn't," replied the doorman. "I see her key over there on the hook."

"I need to talk to her urgently," Jakub said. "Do you have any idea where she might be?"

"No, I don't."

"I saw her a while ago with that trumpeter who's playing here this evening."

"That's right, they say the two of 'em are having an affair. Right now he's probably rehearsing in the social hall."

Dr. Skreta, enthroned on the stage behind his drums, saw Jakub enter and nodded at him. Jakub smiled back and looked over the rows of chairs in which some dozen jazz fans were sitting (yes: Franta—Klima's shadow—was among them). Then Jakub sat down and waited, in the hope that the nurse might appear.

He tried to think where else to look. At this moment she might be in any of a number of places which he knew nothing about. Should he ask the trumpeter? But what could he tell him? Suppose something had happened to her in the meantime? Jakub had already reached the conclusion that if she were to die, her death would be totally incomprehensible and her motiveless murderer would be undetectable. Then why call attention to himself? Why leave a clue, why call suspicion to himself?

But then he reprimanded himself. When a human life is in danger, there is no time for cowardly caution. He took advantage of a pause between two numbers to go backstage. Dr. Skreta turned to him, beaming. Jakub put a finger to his lips and whispered to Skreta to ask the trumpeter if he knew the whereabouts of the nurse he had been sitting with in the restaurant a while back.

"Why are you all so interested in that nurse?" grumbled Skreta. "Where is Ruzena?" he then said loudly to the trumpeter, who blushed and answered he did not know.

"That's too bad. Well, never mind, don't let me interrupt your rehearsal," Jakub said apologetically.

"How do you like our combo?" asked Dr. Skreta.

"It sounds great," replied Jakub, and returned to take a seat in the hall. He knew that he was continuing to behave deplorably. If he really cared about her life, what he should do is raise an alarm and alert everyone to look for her as quickly as possible. But he had been going through the motions of searching for her just to give his conscience an alibi.

In his mind's eye he saw once more the moment when he had handed her the tube containing the poison. Had it really happened so fast that there had been no time to think? Had it really happened without his being aware?

Jakub knew that that was a lie. His conscious mind had not been asleep. He brought to mind once more the face under the blond hair and he realized that his offering her the poison pill had been no accident (no lapse of consciousness), but the fulfillment of an old wish, a longing that had been waiting for years for the right opportunity, a longing so strong that in the end it had created such an opportunity for itself.

Horrified, he rose from his chair and rushed to Marx House. Ruzena was still out.

16

What a pleasant respite and welcome intermission! What a delightful afternoon with three fauns!

What an idyll: both of the trumpeter's ill-starred pursuers sitting at the same table, drinking from the same bottle, happy to be where they were, to have a moment's relief from the necessity of thinking about him. Such touching accord, such harmony!

Mrs. Klima was watching the three young men who had once been her colleagues. She was looking at them as if at a negative of herself: She was a person weighed down by cares, while the trio represented breezy lightheartedness; she was bound to one man, while the three fauns suggested the infinite variety of maleness.

The conversation of the fauns was converging on a specific goal: spending the night with the two women, a night *à cinq*. It was an illusory goal, for they knew that Mrs. Klima's husband was at the spa, but the dream was so beautiful that they were pursuing it despite its unattainability.

Mrs. Klima guessed their inclination and yielded to it, all the more because she recognized that it was only a game of make-believe, only the temptation of fantasy. She laughed at double entendres, joked provocatively with her anonymous woman companion, hoping that this interlude would last and last and thus postpone as long as possible the need to face her rival and to look truth in the eye.

One more bottle of wine, everyone was gay, everyone was drunk, not so much on wine as on their peculiar mood, their desire to prolong the heady, fleeting interlude.

Mrs. Klima felt the director's calf pressing against her left leg. She was perfectly aware of it, but did not withdraw her leg. It was a contact which established a significantly flirtatious connection between them, but at the same time a contact which could have

happened accidentally, a gesture so trivial that she need pay no
attention to it. It was thus a contact precisely on the border between
innocence and immodesty. Kamila did not wish to cross this border,
but she was happy to be able to stay there (on this narrow territory
of unexpected freedom), and she would have been happier still if this
magical frontier moved even further, toward further innuendos,
gestures, and games. Protected by the ambiguous innocence of that
shifting boundary, she longed to let herself be carried beyond the
horizon, on and on.

Inhibited by Kamila's almost painfully radiant beauty, the
director was proceeding slowly, cautiously. In contrast, the more
prosaic charms of Ruzena were exerting a powerful and direct attraction on the cameraman; he was putting his arms around her and
touching her breast.

Kamila was watching. It had been a long time since she last
observed from close quarters the physical intimacy of strangers. She
was watching the male palm covering the girl's breast, rubbing it,
pressing it, stroking it over her dress. She was watching Ruzena's
face, fixed, sensuously resigned, passive. The hand was fondling the
breast, time was sweetly passing, and Kamila felt her other leg
pressed by the assistant's knee.

She said: "I'm in the mood for a little fling tonight."

"The devil take that trumpeter of yours!" said the director.

"The devil take him!" his assistant repeated.

17

At that moment she recognized her. Yes, that's the face from
the photograph her colleague had shown her! Sharply she pushed
away the cameraman's hand.

"What's the matter with you?" he sputtered.

He tried to embrace her once more, and again he was
repulsed.

"How dare you!" she shouted at him.

The director and his assistant laughed. "You really mean it?" the assistant asked her.

"Of course I mean it," she answered sternly.

The assistant glanced at his watch and then said to the cameraman: "It's exactly six o'clock. The new situation has come about because on the stroke of all even hours our friend turns into a puritan. You therefore have to wait until seven."

Another peal of laughter. Ruzena was red with humiliation. She had been caught with a stranger's hand on her breast, she had been caught permitting all sorts of liberties, she had been caught by her greatest enemy while everyone was making fun of her.

The director said to the cameraman: "Perhaps you could ask the young lady to make an exception this one time and accept six as an odd number."

"Do you think there is any theoretical justification for considering six odd?" asked the assistant.

"Definitely," the director replied. "In his famous treatise, Euclid says quite distinctly: 'Under special and very mysterious circumstances, certain even numbers may show odd characteristics.' I have the impression that we are right now face to face with such mysterious circumstances."

"Well, what do you say, Ruzena? Do you agree that we may consider this sixth hour odd?"

Ruzena remained silent.

"Do you consent?" The cameraman leaned toward her.

"The young lady is silent," said the assistant, "and we must therefore decide whether to consider her silence a sign of agreement or opposition."

"We could take a vote," the director said.

"Right," agreed his assistant. "We will vote on the following proposition: We submit that Ruzena's silence be interpreted to mean that in the present exceptional case the number six may rightfully be regarded as odd. Kamila! You're first!"

"I believe that Ruzena is definitely in accord," said Kamila.

"How about you, director?"

"I am convinced," the director said in his gentle voice, "that under the circumstances Ruzena considers six an odd number."

"The cameraman is not a disinterested party, and we will not ask him to vote. As for me, I vote yes," the assistant declared. "We have thus decided by three votes that Ruzena's silence signifies agreement. Cameraman: you are hereby empowered to resume your activity at once."

The cameraman leaned toward Ruzena and put his arm around her in such a way that he was once more touching her breast. Ruzena shoved him away even more violently than before and shrieked: "Keep those filthy paws to yourself!"

"Ruzena, he just likes you a lot, he can't help it. We were all having such a good time . . ." Kamila said soothingly.

Just a few moments earlier Ruzena had been quite passive, abandoning herself to the flow of circumstances, as if she wanted to let her fate be determined by accidental happenings. She would have let herself be seduced, carried away, no matter where, talked into no matter what, just as long as it meant escape from the blind alley in which she had found herself.

However, the unexpected, on which she had pinned her hopes, turned out to be not a promise but a betrayal, and Ruzena —humiliated before her rival and ridiculed by everyone—became aware that she had only one trustworthy support, only one consolation and salvation: the fruit in her womb. Her whole soul (once again! once again!) withdrew inward, into the depths of her body, and she became determined never to part from that being peacefully germinating inside her. This being was her secret triumph which lifted her high above their laughter and their unclean hands. She was bursting to tell it to them, to shout it in their faces, to revenge herself for their ridicule and for that woman's indulgent kindliness.

I must remain calm, she reminded herself, and reached into her handbag for the tube. As she pulled it out, she felt her wrist in the firm grip of someone's hand.

18

Nobody had seen him coming, and suddenly there he was. Ruzena looked up and saw him smiling at her. He continued to hold her hand; she felt the firmness of his grip and yielded; the tube dropped back into the depth of the handbag.

"Ladies and gentlemen, permit me to join you. My name is Bartleff."

None of the men around the table was overjoyed by the stranger's arrival, none of them bothered to introduce himself, and Ruzena lacked the social poise necessary to take over these amenities.

"I see that my arrival has upset you," Bartleff said. He took a nearby chair and pushed it toward the head of the table, so that he was facing the entire company and had Ruzena at his right. "Forgive me," he continued, "I have the peculiar habit of appearing rather than arriving."

"In that case," the assistant retorted, "you will permit us to consider you a mere appearance to which we need not pay any attention."

"I gladly give you my permission," Bartleff replied with a slight bow. "But I am afraid that in spite of all your best efforts you will not succeed."

He then turned toward the lighted door of the kitchen and clapped his hands.

"Who invited you to sit with us, anyway?" said the cameraman.

"Are you trying to tell me that I am not welcome? Ruzena and I could leave right now, but habits are hard to break. I generally sit at this table of an afternoon and have a glass of wine." He examined the label of the bottle standing on the table. "Of course, I insist on something better than that!"

"I'd love to know how you find any decent wine in this hole," said the assistant.

"You seem to be quite a show-off, mister," the cameraman said, and eager to ridicule the uninvited guest he added: "Of course, by a certain age there's little left for a man except showing off."

"You're wrong," said Bartleff as if he had not heard the cameraman's insult, "in this restaurant they have better wines stashed away than in some of the most expensive hotels."

A moment later he was shaking the hand of the innkeeper, who had not bothered to show himself earlier but was now bowing to Bartleff and inquiring: "Shall I set the table for six?"

"Naturally," Bartleff replied, and turned to his guests: "Ladies and gentlemen, I am inviting you to share with me some wine which I have tasted many times before and invariably found excellent. Will you do me the honor?"

Nobody replied, and the innkeeper said: "If I may say so, when it comes to food and drink I can assure you you can have complete trust in Mr. Bartleff."

"My friend," Bartleff said to the innkeeper, "bring us two bottles and a big plate of cheese." Then he turned once more to the others. "There is no reason for you to be uneasy. Any friends of Ruzenka are friends of mine."

A boy hardly twelve years old came trotting out of the kitchen carrying a tray with glasses, plates, and napkins. He put it down on a nearby table and proceeded to remove the old glasses, which he placed on the tray together with the half-empty bottle of wine. He carefully wiped the soiled tabletop with a napkin and spread a gleaming white tablecloth. He picked up the old glasses again and was about to place them one by one before the guests.

"Forget about those dirty glasses and that old vinegar," Bartleff said to the boy. "Daddy is bringing us real wine."

The cameraman protested: "Mister, would you mind very much letting us drink what we please?"

"Just as you wish, my good fellow," Bartleff replied. "I don't like forcing happiness on people. Everybody has a right to his lousy wine, to his stupidity, and to his dirty fingernails. Listen, son," he turned to the boy, "put the old glasses on the table after all, and the old bottle, too. My guests shall be free to choose between wine bred in fogs and wine born of the sun."

Soon they each had two glasses before them: one clean and one containing traces of the old wine. The innkeeper approached the table with two bottles, squeezed the first between his knees, and with a strong tug pulled out the cork. He poured a small sample into Bartleff's glass. Bartleff lifted the glass to his lips, took a sip, and turned to the innkeeper. "Excellent. Twenty-three?"

"Twenty-two," the innkeeper replied.

"You may pour," said Bartleff, and the innkeeper circled the table filling all the clean glasses.

Bartleff delicately lifted his glass by the stem. "My friends, please taste this wine. It has the sweet taste of the past. Savor it as if you were sucking the marrow of a long-forgotten summer. By means of this toast I would like to join the past with the present, the sun of nineteen twenty-two with the sun of this moment. That sun is Ruzena, that modest and simple girl who is a queen without realizing it. She shines against the backdrop of this provincial place like a jewel on a beggar's coat. She is like the moon forgotten by the pale sky of the day. She is like a butterfly over a plain of snow."

The cameraman attempted a forced laugh. "Aren't you overdoing it, mister?"

"No, I am not," replied Bartleff, facing the cameraman. "It seems so only to you, because you are always living below the level of true existence, you bitter weed, you anthropomorphized vat of vinegar! You're full of acid, which bubbles inside you like an alchemist's brew. Your highest wish is to be able to see all around you the same ugliness you carry inside yourself. That's the only way you can feel for a few moments some kind of peace between yourself and the world. That's because the world, which is beautiful, seems horrible to you, torments you and excludes you. How unbearable it must be to have dirty fingernails while a beautiful woman is sitting next to you! It is necessary for you to besmirch the woman before you can derive any pleasure from her. Am I right, my good man? I am glad you are hiding your hands under the table; obviously I must have hit on the truth when I talked about dirty nails."

"I don't give a shit for propriety, I am not a clown like you with your starched collar and fancy cravat," the cameraman snapped.

"Your dirty nails and torn sweater are nothing new under the sun," said Bartleff. "A long time ago a certain Cynic philosopher proudly paraded around Athens in a moth-eaten coat, hoping that everyone would admire his contempt for convention. When Socrates met him, he said: *Through the hole in your coat I see your vanity.* Your dirt, too, dear sir, is self-indulgent and your self-indulgence is dirty."

Ruzena could hardly get over her stunned surprise. A man whom she had known only casually as one of the patients had suddenly appeared like a gallant knight. She was bewitched by the elegant ease of his behavior and the vigorous skill with which he had vanquished the cameraman's arrogance.

"I see that you've lost your tongue," Bartleff said to the cameraman after a few moments of silence. "Please believe that I had no wish to hurt you. I love harmony and dislike quarrels, and if I was carried away by eloquence please accept my apology. All I really want is to have you taste this wine and to join me in a toast to Ruzenka, for whose sake I am here."

Bartleff once more lifted his glass, but nobody joined him.

"Mr. Innkeeper," said Bartleff, "be good enough to drink a toast with us!"

"With wine like this it's always a pleasure," responded the innkeeper, picking up a clean glass from a neighboring table and filling it. "Mr. Bartleff is an expert on good wine. He sniffed out my cellar and made straight for it like a swallow for its nest."

Bartleff laughed the happy laugh of a flattered man.

"Will you toast Ruzenka with us?"

"Ruzenka?" asked the innkeeper.

"Yes, Ruzenka," Bartleff said, bowing his head in her direction. "Do you like her as much as I do?"

"Mr. Bartleff, you're always surrounded by beautiful women. With my eyes closed I'd know perfectly well that this young lady must be beautiful, just because she is sitting next to you."

Bartleff once more broke into happy laughter, the innkeeper laughed too, and, oddly enough, so did Kamila, who had found Bartleff amusing from the very first. This laughter was unexpected and strangely, inexplicably contagious. Out of courteous solidarity the director joined Kamila in laughing, he was soon joined by his assistant, and finally Ruzena broke down too; blissfully plunging into the many-voiced merriment. It was her first carefree, relaxed moment of the whole day. She laughed loudest of all and could not get her fill of mirth.

Bartleff offered a toast: "To Ruzenka!" The innkeeper lifted his glass, and so did Kamila and the director and his assistant, and all of them repeated after Bartleff: "To Ruzenka!" Even the cameraman lifted his glass and silently swallowed a gulp.

The director savored a sip and said: "This is really superb!"

"I told you," grinned the innkeeper.

In the meantime the boy had placed in the middle of the table a plate heaped with assorted cheeses, and Bartleff said: "Help yourselves, they're excellent!"

The director remarked in surprise: "What a fabulous selection! I feel I am back in France!"

By now the tension had completely disappeared. They all chatted and joked, sampled all the cheeses and wondered how in the world the innkeeper managed to get hold of them (in a country where cheese is usually limited to a few standard varieties), and kept refilling their glasses over and over.

Just as they were all enjoying themselves to the utmost, Bartleff rose to his feet with a small bow: "It was good to be in your company and I thank you. My friend Doctor Skreta is having a concert this evening, and Ruzenka and I wish to hear it."

19

Bartleff walked off with Ruzena into the light mist of approaching sundown, and the high spirits that had promised to waft the revelers to a fabulous island of illicit pleasures gradually vanished beyond any possible hope of return. Everyone suddenly felt very let down.

Mrs. Klima felt as if she had been expelled from a dream in which she would have dearly loved to remain. She had been thinking that actually there was no need to go to the concert at all. She had toyed with the idea of how fantastically surprised she herself would have been suddenly to learn that she had come to the spa in pursuit not of her husband but of adventure. How beautiful it would have been to stay with those three filmmakers and to return home in the morning. Something kept telling her that this was the thing for her to do: a deliberate action, an act of liberation, a way of healing herself, of breaking the spell she was under.

But now she was already too sober. All magic charms had evaporated. She was again alone with herself, her past, her heavy head full of old tormenting thoughts. She longed to extend that brief dream by at least a few more hours, but she knew that the dream was already fading like the glimmering twilight.

"I'll have to be going, too," she said.

They tried to talk her out of leaving, but realized they no longer had sufficient persuasiveness or self-confidence to make her stay.

"Shit!" said the cameraman. "Who was that man, anyway?"

They wanted to ask the innkeeper, but from the moment Bartleff had left nobody paid any further attention to them. From inside the restaurant came the noise of inebriated guests, and the crew with Kamila sat forlornly in the garden with their half-finished wine and platter of cheese.

"Whoever he was, he spoiled our party. He took one of our beautiful women, and the other one is about to leave us, too. Let's escort Kamila."

"No," said Kamila. "Please stay. I want to go by myself."

She was no longer with them. Their presence was beginning to annoy her. Jealousy had come for her as suddenly and surely as death. She was in its power and nothing else mattered. She rose to her feet and set out in the direction that Bartleff and Ruzena had taken. From a distance she heard the cameraman's voice: "Shit . . ."

20

Before the beginning of the concert Jakub and Olga stopped by the small dressing room set aside for the performers to wish Skreta good luck. Then they took their seats in the hall. Olga was hoping they would leave during intermission so that she and Jakub could spend the rest of the evening together undisturbed. Jakub objected that his friend Skreta might take their early departure amiss, but Olga maintained that he would not even notice it.

The hall was almost filled, and they took the last two seats in their row.

"That woman has been following me all day like a shadow," Olga whispered to Jakub as they sat down.

Jakub glanced over his shoulder and saw that just a few seats away sat Bartleff and next to him the nurse with the fateful tube in her handbag. His heart skipped a beat but because of a lifetime's practice in concealing his inner states he said quite calmly: "I see that ours is the row of free tickets which Skreta handed out to friends. That means that he knows where we're sitting and he'll notice if we leave."

"You can tell him that the acoustics were bad in this part of the hall and that we switched to another section," said Olga.

At that point Klima appeared on the stage carrying a golden trumpet and the audience broke into applause. He was followed by Dr. Skreta. There was an even greater burst of applause and a wave of rustling excitement swept through the hall. Dr. Skreta, standing modestly behind the trumpeter, made a clumsy gesture with his arm, intended to indicate that the real star of the concert was the guest from the capital. The charming awkwardness of the gesture did not escape the attention of the audience, which responded with a still louder ovation. From the back someone shouted: "Long live our Dr. Skreta!"

The pianist, the least striking or acclaimed member of the trio, sat down at the keyboard, Skreta enthroned himself behind an imposing array of drums, and the trumpeter strode across the stage with a springy, rhythmic step.

The applause had already died down, the pianist had played a few chords and launched into his solo introduction, but Jakub saw that his physician friend was flustered and looking anxiously around. The trumpeter, too, noticed the doctor's uneasiness and stepped closer. Skreta whispered something and then the two of them bent over and began to scan the floor, until at last the trumpeter picked up a drumstick which had rolled to the foot of the piano and handed it to Skreta.

The audience, which had been intently watching the whole scene, burst into new applause. The pianist, thinking that the accolade was in appreciation of his introductory passages, continued to play while bowing his head in acknowledgment.

Olga touched Jakub's arm and whispered: "It's beautiful! It's so beautiful that I believe this moment marks the end of my streak of bad luck!"

At last the piano was joined by the trumpet and drums. Klima was blowing in rhythm to his springy steps across the floor, and Skreta sat behind his drums like an exalted Buddha.

Jakub tried to imagine what it would be like if the nurse suddenly decided to take a pill in the middle of the concert, swallowed it, collapsed in an agony of convulsions, and slumped dead in her seat while on stage Dr. Skreta continued to pound the drums to the cheers and applause of the public.

And in a flash it became clear to him why that girl had drawn a ticket in the same row as he: the unexpected encounter in the restaurant earlier in the day had been a temptation, a trial. It had occurred for the sole purpose of showing him his true self: poisoner of a fellow human being. But the author of this trial (the God in whose existence he did not believe) did not exact a bloody sacrifice, required no innocent blood. The trial would not end in death but in Jakub's self-discovery, in deliverance from sinful moral arrogance. That was why the nurse was now sitting in the same row, so that he could still save her at the last moment. And that was why her companion happened to be a man who had become his friend and who surely would help him.

Yes, he would wait for the first opportunity, perhaps the first break between numbers, and he would ask Bartleff to step out into the lobby with Ruzena. There he would make some sort of explanation and the whole unbelievable madness would come to an end.

The musicians finished the first number, there was applause, the nurse said "Excuse me" and accompanied by Bartleff pushed her way into the aisle. Jakub was about to get to his feet and follow them but Olga caught him by the hand and held him back. "No, please, not now. Wait until intermission."

It had all happened faster than he was able to realize. The musicians launched into the next number and Jakub understood that the One who was testing him had placed Ruzena in a nearby seat not in order to save him but in order to destroy him and to establish his guilt beyond all doubt.

The trumpeter kept on blowing lustily, Dr. Skreta loomed behind him like a mighty Buddha at the drums, and Jakub sat paralyzed, seeing neither the trumpeter nor the doctor. He saw only himself, he saw himself sitting paralyzed and he could not tear his sight from this horrible image.

21

The first ringing tones of his beloved trumpet made Klima feel that he was alone onstage, filling the entire hall with sound. He felt strong, unconquerable. Ruzena was sitting in the complimentary row of seats next to Bartleff (that, too, seemed like a sudden good omen), and everything was humming with cheering vibrations. The public was listening eagerly and its obvious approval reinforced Klima's optimistic mood. At the sound of the first wave of applause Klima pointed with a graceful gesture toward Dr. Skreta, who for some reason was becoming increasingly dear to him that evening. The doctor stood up and took a bow.

But in the course of the second number, as Klima looked into the audience, he noticed that the chair on which Ruzena had been sitting was empty. That disturbed him. From that instant he played uneasily while scanning the hall seat by seat and failing to find her. It occurred to him that she might have left on purpose in order to avoid further conversation with him, having made up her mind not to appear before the abortion commission. Where was he to look for her after the concert? And what if he failed to find her?

He sensed that he was playing poorly, mechanically, absentmindedly. However, his lackluster performance was not noticed by the public, which was satisfied and kept breaking into ever louder ovations after each piece.

He tried to console himself with the thought that she might have just gone to the toilet. Perhaps she had a touch of malaise, as often happens to pregnant women. When she had been absent almost half an hour, he told himself that she might have gone home to fetch something and would soon reappear in her seat. But intermission had come and gone, the concert was nearing its end, and her seat was still empty. Perhaps she did not dare enter the hall in the middle of a number? Would she appear after the next wave of applause?

But the applause had died down and Ruzena was nowhere to be seen. Klima was getting desperate. The audience was giving him a standing ovation and shouting for encores. Klima turned toward Dr. Skreta and shook his head to indicate that he did not feel like playing anymore. But he was met by a pair of shining eyes that yearned to continue drumming, on and on, all night long.

The audience took Klima's gesture of refusal as the customary coquetry of a star, and clapped more and more. At that moment a beautiful young woman pushed her way into the front row. When Klima saw her he thought he was going to faint. She was smiling at him, saying (he could not hear her voice, but he read the words on her lips): "Go on, play! Please play!"

Klima lifted his trumpet as a signal that he would do another number. The audience at once became hushed.

Klima's two fellow musicians beamed and launched into the encore. Klima felt as if he were playing in a funeral band, marching behind his own coffin. He played and he knew that all was lost, that there was nothing left to do but close his eyes, cross his arms over his chest, and let the wheels of fate roll over him.

22

On the top of Bartleff's liquor cabinet were arrayed numerous bottles with ornate foreign labels. Ruzena was not familiar with such luxuries, and she asked for whiskey only because that was the one word that came to her mind.

At the same time, she tried to think her way through the daze that had enveloped her and to make sense of the situation. She had asked him several times what made him seek her out when actually he hardly knew her. "I want to know. I want to know," she kept repeating, "why you suddenly decided to see me."

"I've been wanting to do it for a long time," Bartleff answered, gazing into her eyes.

"But why today, of all days?"

"Because everything has its own proper time. And our time had come today."

Those words sounded mysterious, but Ruzena felt that they had the ring of truth. The hopelessness of her situation had this day really become so unbearable that something had to happen.

"Yes," she said pensively, "today was a special day."

"Surely you agree that I arrived just at the right time," Bartleff said in a velvety voice.

Ruzena felt a vague, enormously sweet sense of relief: If Bartleff appeared precisely at the right moment, this must mean that everything that was happening was directed from the outside after all, and she could relax and put herself in the hands of this higher power.

"It's true, you really did come at the right time."

"I know."

And yet there was still something she did not understand: "But why?"

"Because I love you."

These words came out very softly, and yet they seemed to fill the room.

Her voice, too, became hushed: "You love me?"

"Yes, I do."

Both Franta and Klima had used the word *love*, but it was not until now that she heard it as it really sounds when it comes, unexpected, unasked for, naked. It had entered the room like a miracle. It was totally inexplicable, but for all that it seemed all the more real to her, because the most basic things in life exist without explanation and without cause, containing their own reason within themselves.

"Really?" she asked, and her voice—normally rather strident —sounded like a whisper.

"Really."

"But I'm just a completely ordinary girl."

"No, you're not."

"Yes, I am."

"You're beautiful."

"No, I'm not."

"You're gentle."

"No." She shook her head.

"You radiate kindness and goodness."

"No, no, no." She kept shaking her head.

"I know what you're like. I know it better than you do."

"You don't know me."

"Yes, I do."

The trust emanating from Bartleff's eyes was like a magic balm, and Ruzena yearned for that loving gaze to bathe and nestle her as long as possible.

"Am I really like that?"

"Yes, you are. I know it."

It was beautiful to the point of vertigo; in his eyes she felt herself fine, gentle, pure, noble as a queen. She felt herself filled with honey and fragrant herbs. She could easily have fallen in love with herself. (God, she had never felt that way before, so sweetly pleased with her own self!)

"But you hardly know me!" she continued to protest.

"I have known you a long time. I've been watching you for a long time but you never suspected it. I know you by heart." His fingertips caressed her face. "Your nose, your smile—so lightly drawn, your hair . . ."

He started to undress her and she did not resist, she kept looking into his eyes, into his gaze which bathed her like a sweet, clear stream. She sat facing him, her bare breasts swelling under his gaze, longing to be seen and praised. Her whole body turned toward his eyes like a sunflower toward the sun.

23

They sat in Jakub's room. Olga was talking about something and Jakub kept reminding himself that there still was time to act: he could go once more to Marx House and if she wasn't there he could call on Bartleff in the neighboring apartment and ask him if he knew where she was.

Olga kept on talking and in the meantime he was thinking ahead to the painful scene that would ensue if he were to find the nurse—mumbling, stuttering, apologizing, trying to get her to return the pill. Suddenly, as if exhausted by these visions with which he had been struggling for several hours, he felt an intense apathy taking hold of him.

It was not apathy born merely of fatigue, it was a conscious, belligerent indifference. Jakub became aware that he did not give a hoot whether that creature with blond hair lived or died, and that it would actually be nothing but hypocrisy and unseemly travesty if he tried to save her. He would actually be deceiving the One Who was testing him. For the One testing him (the nonexistent God) wished to learn what Jakub was really like and not what he pretended to be like. And Jakub decided to be honest in the face of his examiner; to be the person he really was.

They sat in their armchairs, facing each other with a small table between them. Jakub saw Olga leaning toward him across the table, he heard her voice: "I want to kiss you. How come we have known each other such a long time but have never kissed?"

24

A forced smile on her face, jittery and nervous, that was how Mrs. Klima elbowed her way to the performers' lounge to see her husband. She was terrified by the idea of looking at the actual face of his mistress. But no mistress was to be seen. A couple of young girls hovered around Klima, pleading for autographs, but she immediately discerned (her eye could be as keen as a hawk's) that none of them knew him personally.

All the same, she was convinced that a mistress was not far off. She knew it from Klima's face, which was pale and distracted, from his smile, as forced as hers.

Dr. Skreta, the pharmacist, and several other people, most likely doctors and their wives, greeted her and introduced themselves. Somebody suggested that they go across the street to the only bar that was still open. Klima objected that he was too tired. It occurred to Mrs. Klima that his mistress was probably waiting in the bar and that this was the reason for her husband's opposition. Because disaster always attracted her like a magnet, she begged him, for her sake, to change his mind.

But the bar, too, failed to disclose any woman whom she might suspect of being connected with him. They sat down at a large table. Dr. Skreta was loquacious and praised the trumpeter to the skies. The pharmacist was full of shy, inarticulate happiness. Mrs. Klima tried to be chatty and charming. "You were simply marvelous, Doctor," she said to Skreta, "and you, too, my dear pharmacist. The whole atmosphere was sincere, gay, carefree—a thousand times more enjoyable than concerts in the capital."

Without looking at him directly, she did not lose track of him for a single second. She sensed that he was trying extremely hard to cover up his nervousness, and that he made a remark now and then only to conceal that his mind was elsewhere. It was clear to her that her arrival had spoiled some plan of his, and not an unimportant one at that. If it had been only a matter of some routine adventure (Klima always swore to her that he could never fall in love with another woman), the situation certainly would not have given rise to such deep upset. She had not seen his mistress, but she was certain that she was seeing his infatuation (a suffering, desperate infatuation), and this sight was perhaps even more tormenting.

"What's the matter with you, Mr. Klima?" suddenly exclaimed the pharmacist, a man whose quiet demeanor was linked to great kindliness and sensitivity.

"It's nothing, nothing at all," replied the trumpeter. "I just have a bit of a headache."

"Would you like an analgesic?" asked the pharmacist.

"No, no, thank you." Klima shook his head. "But please forgive me if we leave a little earlier after all. I really am very tired."

25

How did she finally find the courage to do it?

From the very moment she had joined Jakub in the restaurant he seemed different. He was laconic yet agreeable, distracted yet reasonably attentive, his mind was somewhere else and yet he did everything she wanted. It was precisely his distractedness (she ascribed it to his imminent departure) that she found pleasant: she was speaking her words to his absent face, as if she were speaking into a void where she could not be heard. She could thus say things she had never said to him before.

Now, in asking him for a kiss, it seemed to her that she disturbed and frightened him. But this did not deter her, on the contrary, even that was pleasant: at last she felt like that daring, provocative woman she had always longed to be, a woman who controls the situation, sets it in motion, watches her partner with curiosity, and disconcerts him.

She continued to look him firmly in the eye and said with a smile: "But not here. It would be ridiculous for us to kiss leaning over a table. Come on."

She took him by the hand, led him over to the couch, and relished the wit, elegance, and calm self-assurance of her own behavior. She kissed him with a passion she had not known before. It was not the spontaneous passion of a body unable to control itself, it was the passion of the brain, conscious and voluntary. She wanted to tear from Jakub the mantle of his paternal role, to shock him and at the same time titillate herself by the sight of his confusion, she wanted to seduce him and watch herself in the act of seduction, to learn the taste of his tongue and feel his paternal hands gradually daring to explore her body.

She unbuttoned his jacket and pulled it off with a firm tug.

26

He kept his eyes glued on him throughout the concert and afterward mingled with the throng of autograph hunters enthusiastically pushing their way toward the stage. But Ruzena was not there. He then trailed a group of people who were leading the trumpeter to the local tavern and followed them inside, convinced that Ruzena was there waiting for the musician. But he was wrong. He stepped out into the street again, and for a long time patrolled the entrance of the tavern.

He felt a sudden pang: the trumpeter emerged from the bar with a female figure pressed close to him. He was absolutely convinced that it was Ruzena, but it turned out to be someone else.

He followed them to Richmond House. Klima and the unknown woman disappeared inside.

He quickly crossed the park toward Marx House. The doors were still unlocked. He asked the doorman whether Ruzena had returned yet and was told that she had not.

He ran back to Richmond, worried that Ruzena might have joined Klima there in the meantime. He walked back and forth along the park road, watching the entrance. He did not understand what was happening. All kinds of ideas ran through his mind, but he was determined to concentrate on one task: to keep a sharp lookout, to watch and wait until one of them appeared.

Why? What purpose did this watch serve? Wouldn't he be better off going home to bed?

He had decided that he must learn the truth at last.

But did he really want to know the truth? Did he really wish to learn beyond any doubt that Ruzena was sleeping with Klima? Did he not, on the contrary, yearn to find some evidence of Ruzena's innocence? But in his suspicious frame of mind, would he trust such evidence?

He did not really know what he was waiting for. He knew only that he was ready to wait a long time, the whole night if necessary, even many nights. A jealous person finds time streaming by with incredible speed. Jealousy fills the mind more completely than the most absorbing mental task. Not a single second is free; the victim of jealousy never knows boredom.

Franta kept patrolling his stretch of road, barely one hundred steps long, from which the entrance of Richmond House was visible. He is about to walk back and forth this way all night, while everyone else is asleep, he is destined to keep marching until the break of day, until the start of the next section.

Why doesn't he at least sit down? There is a row of benches facing Richmond House!

He cannot sit still. Jealousy is like a bad toothache. It does not let a person do anything, not even sit still. It can only be walked off. Back and forth, back and forth.

27

They followed the route taken earlier by Bartleff and Ruzena, Jakub and Olga: up the stairs to the second floor, and then along the red plush carpet to the end of the corridor. The entrance to Bartleff's apartment was straight ahead, Jakub's room was to the right.

The room Dr. Skreta had assigned to Klima was on the left. He opened the door and turned on the light, aware of Kamila's quick searching glance around the room. He knew that glance: she was searching for traces of a woman. He knew all about her. He knew that the affection she was showing him was not sincere, that she had come to spy on him, that she was about to pretend that she had come to give him a happy surprise. And he knew that for her part, she was well aware of his bad humor and was convinced that she had spoiled some amorous intrigue of his.

"Darling, are you sure you don't mind that I came?" she said.

"Why should I mind?"

"I thought you might be lonely here."

"It was kind of lonesome without you. It was good to see you out there in the audience, cheering me on."

"You seem a little tired. Or is something bothering you?"

"No, nothing is bothering me. I'm just tired, that's all."

"You're irritable because you were surrounded by a bunch of men, and that always depresses you. But now you are with a beautiful woman. Do you think I am a beautiful woman?"

"Yes, I certainly do," answered Klima, and those were the first sincere words he had said to her that day. Kamila was divinely beautiful, and it pained Klima immensely that such beauty was exposed to mortal peril. But this incarnation of loveliness was now laughing at him, beginning to disrobe. He gazed at her emerging body as if he were about to say farewell to it forever. The breasts, those beautiful, pure, faultless breasts, the narrow waist, the smooth hips, which had just slipped free of panties. He gazed at her mournfully, as if she were a memory, as if she were behind glass, far away. Her nudity seemed so distant from him that he did not feel the slightest excitement. And yet he devoured her with his eyes. He drank in her nakedness as a condemned man drains his last cup. He drank her nakedness as a man drinks his lost past, his lost life.

Kamila drew close to him. "What's the matter? Aren't you going to take your clothes off?"

He had no choice but to disrobe, and he felt terribly sad.

"Tiredness is no excuse, sir. I came all the way out here just to be with you. And I'm in the mood for love."

He knew that it was not true. He knew that Kamila did not have the slightest desire to make love and was forcing herself to act provocative only because she recognized his melancholy and ascribed it to frustrated love for another woman. He knew (Good Lord, how well he knew her!) that her seductive behavior was only an act to test how strongly his interest was committed elsewhere, and to torment herself with his indifference.

"I really am exhausted," he said.

She embraced him and then led him to the bed. "You'll see how quickly I'll make you feel better," she said, and began to toy with his naked body.

He was stretched out on the bed as if it were an operating table. He knew that all his wife's efforts would prove futile. He shrank into himself. Kamila's moist mouth was sliding all over him, he knew that she wanted to torment both herself and him, and he hated her. He hated her with all the enormity of his love: It was all her fault, it was her jealousy, her spying, her mistrust, her surprise visit that spoiled everything, that caused their marriage to be jeopardized by an explosive bomb nesting in a strange woman's belly, a bomb timed to explode in seven months and blow everything to pieces. It was she, with her insane anxiety about love, who had destroyed it all.

She put her mouth to his lap and he felt his organ retreating under her caress, fleeing from her, becoming small and tremulous.

And he knew that Kamila interpreted his physical rejection of her as a sign of his infatuation with another woman. He knew that she was suffering terribly, and that the more she suffered the more her moist lips would continue to torment his incapable body.

28

The last thing he ever wanted to do was make love to this girl. He was eager to make her happy and to surround her with kindness, but this kindness had nothing in common with physical love, in fact it excluded erotic desire, for it longed to be pure, altruistic, dissociated from any enjoyment.

But what was he to do now? Should he reject Olga for the sake of the continuing purity of his benevolence? He knew that this would be wrong; his rejection would hurt Olga, perhaps leave permanent scars. He realized that he must drink the cup of kindness to the very bottom.

And then suddenly she was standing naked before him and he told himself that her face was noble and kind. But that bit of encouragement meant little as soon as he perceived the face together with the rest of the body, which looked like a long thin stalk topped with an inordinately large, hairy flower.

But no matter what she looked like, Jakub realized that there was no escape. Moreover, he felt that his body (that slavish body) was once again lifting its obliging spear. It seemed to him, however, as if this excitement was happening in somebody else, far away, outside his own self, as if he was getting excited without his own participation, quietly contemptuous of it all. His soul was far from his body, contemplating the poison in a stranger's handbag, and only dimly aware of the body's deplorably blind, selfish pursuit of its trivial interests.

A fleeting memory passed through Jakub's mind: He had been about ten years old when he first learned how children came into the world, and the idea of the birth process obsessed him more and more as he gradually gained a more detailed and concrete knowledge of female anatomy. He often tried to visualize his own birth. He imagined his tiny body sliding through a narrow, damp tunnel, his nose and mouth full of slime. That mucus smeared him, marked him. Yes, that female secretion penetrated so deeply that throughout the course of Jakub's life it exerted its secret power over him, summoning him at will and ruling the various mysterious mechanisms of his body. He had always felt a distaste for this humiliation, and he resisted it at least to the extent that he never gave his soul to women, that he safeguarded his freedom and solitude, and that he restricted the "reign of mucus" to certain limited hours of his life. Yes, perhaps this was the reason he liked Olga so much: for him, she was a being totally beyond the bounds of sex, whose body would never remind him of the humiliating manner of his birth.

He made himself chase these thoughts away, because in the meantime the situation on the couch was progressing rapidly, he was about to penetrate her, and he did not wish to do so while such distasteful thoughts were in his mind. He reminded himself that this woman opening up to him was a being to whom he had dedicated the only pure love of his life; his sole purpose in now making love to her was to make her happy, to give her pleasure, to make her cheerful and self-confident.

But he was in for a surprise: he found himself floating on top of her as if carried along by waves of well-being. He felt happy. His soul humbly identified with the activity of his body, as if lovemaking was but a physical expression of kind, loving, pure feelings toward another being. All obstacles vanished, nothing rang false. They held each other tight and their breath mingled.

Those were long, beautiful minutes and then Olga whispered a lascivious word in his ear. She whispered it once, then once more, excited by her own boldness.

The waves of well-being receded at once, and Jakub and the girl found themselves stranded in a desert.

This was an unusual reaction for Jakub. Generally, when he

made love he had no objection to lascivious talk. In fact, it stimulated his sensuality and aggressiveness, and safely estranged the woman from his soul while making her pleasantly desirable to his body. But coming from Olga's mouth, the coarse word totally destroyed his illusions. It woke him from a dream. The mist of loving kindness evaporated and suddenly the girl in his arms appeared just as he had seen her at the beginning: a big flower of a head on top of a thin, trembling stalk of a body. That pitiful creature was behaving as provocatively as a harlot, without ceasing to be pitiful, so that her suggestive words sounded ridiculous and sad.

But Jakub knew he must not reveal that there was anything wrong; he had to keep playing the game, he had to continue draining the bitter cup of kindness to the bottom, because this absurd embrace was his one good deed, his sole claim to redemption (not for an instant did he forget the poison pill), his only salvation.

29

Like a large pearl glistening in a gray oyster shell, Bartleff's luxurious apartment was surrounded on both sides by the modest, plain rooms assigned to Jakub and Klima. Both of these rooms had already been peacefully quiet for a long time, as Ruzena was still blissfully sobbing her last gasps of delight in Bartleff's arms.

Then she lay quietly by his side while he gently stroked her face. After a while she broke into tears. She cried for a long time, her head buried on his chest.

Bartleff cuddled her like a little girl and she really did feel like a child. Small as never before (she had never tried to lose herself on anyone's bosom before), but also big as never before (she had never felt so much joy before). And each sob was a new name for the feeling of bliss she had never experienced before.

Where was Klima now, and where was Franta? They were somewhere in a distant haze, figures as light as feathers, floating toward the horizon. And where was her stubborn yearning to get rid of one and capture the other? Where was her anger, the aggrieved silence she had been spinning around herself all day like a cocoon?

Her sobs gradually subsided as he kept on stroking her face. He told her to go to sleep. He had his own bed in the adjoining room. Ruzena opened her eyes and watched him: naked, Bartleff went to the bathroom (the sound of running water could be heard), then he returned, opened a closet, pulled out a blanket, and gently covered her.

Ruzena saw the knotted veins in his calves. When he bent over she noticed that his wavy, graying hair was thin and that the scalp was showing through. Yes, Bartleff was in his fifties, and somewhat paunchy at that, but Ruzena did not mind. On the contrary, his age reassured her, brought out her youthfulness in a dazzling new light so that she no longer felt gray and formless but full of a sense of vitality, a sense that her life's journey was only beginning. In his presence she now realized that her youth would not fade for a long time to come, that there was no need to hurry, no need to fear the passage of time. Bartleff once again sat down by her side, held her, and she had the feeling that not only was she safely snuggled in the soothing embrace of his arms, but in the comforting embrace of his years.

Her consciousness dimmed and she abandoned herself to a confused play of fantasy. Then she woke and it seemed to her that the whole room was bathed by a peculiar bluish light. She had never seen such a strange glow before. What was it? Had the moon come down to earth wrapped in a bluish gown? Or was she dreaming with her eyes open?

Bartleff continued to smile at her and to stroke her face.

At last she closed her eyes, carried away by a dream.

Fifth
Day

1

It was still dark, and Klima awoke from a very light sleep. He wanted to catch Ruzena before she left for work. But how to explain to Kamila the need to rush off before daybreak?

He looked at his watch: five o'clock. He knew that unless he got up quickly he would miss Ruzena, but he could think of no excuse. His heart pounded with excitement. It could not be helped. He got up and started to dress, quietly so as not to wake Kamila. He was just buttoning his jacket when he heard her voice. It was a high-pitched, half-awake little voice: "Where are you going?"

He stepped to her bed and kissed her lightly on the mouth. "Go back to sleep, I won't be gone long."

"I'll go with you," said Kamila, but drifted back into sleep. Klima quickly walked out the door.

2

Was it possible? Could he still be patrolling back and forth? Yes. But now he stopped. He saw Klima stepping out of Richmond House. He waited a few moments and then followed him quietly toward Marx House. He passed through the lobby (the doorman was asleep) and hid in a corner of the corridor leading to Ruzena's room. He saw the trumpeter knocking on her door. The door remained closed. Klima knocked a few more times, then turned and walked away.

Franta followed him out of the building. He saw him striding down the long avenue toward the baths, where Ruzena was due to begin her shift in half an hour. He ran into Marx House, pounded on Ruzena's door, and whispered loudly into the keyhole: "It's me! Franta! Don't be scared! Open up!"

There was no answer.

As he was leaving, the doorman was just waking up.

"Is Ruzena at home?" Franta asked him.

"She hasn't been back since yesterday," the doorman said.

Franta stepped out into the street. In the distance he saw Klima entering the bathhouse.

3

Ruzena regularly woke at five-thirty. She did not sleep any longer this morning, even though she had fallen asleep under such blissful circumstances. She got up, dressed, and tiptoed into the adjoining room.

Bartleff was lying on his side, breathing heavily, and his hair, which was normally neatly combed, was tousled, revealing a patch of bald scalp. In sleep, his face looked grayer and older. On his night table stood an array of medicines which reminded Ruzena of a hospital. But none of this bothered her. She gazed on him and felt tears rising to her eyes. She had never known a more beautiful night. She had a strange desire to kneel down before him. She did not do so, but she leaned over and kissed him lightly on the forehead.

As she was nearing the baths she saw Franta striding toward her.

A day earlier, such an encounter would have troubled her. Even though she was in love with the trumpeter, Franta meant a great deal to her. He and Klima formed an indivisible pair: one signified everyday reality, the other a dream; one wanted her, the other did not; she wanted to escape from one and longed for the other. Each of them determined the existential meaning of the other. Her decision that the father of her baby was Klima did not erase Franta from her life. On the contrary: it was precisely Franta who had moved her to this decision. She oscillated between them as if they were the two poles of her existence; they were the north and south poles of the only planet she knew.

But this morning she suddenly realized that this universe contained other worlds, and that it was possible to live without Klima and without Franta, too. She discovered that there was no need to hurry; that a wise, mature man was capable of leading her into a realm where time was kinder and youth did not wither so fast.

"Where were you last night?" Franta lashed out.

"None of your business."

"I was at your house. You weren't home."

"It's none of your business where I was," said Ruzena, and without stopping she walked through the bathhouse gate. "And stop following me."

Franta remained standing alone in front of the building, and because his legs ached from his all-night vigil he sat down on a bench from which he could keep an eye on the entrance.

Ruzena hurried up the stairs and entered the large second-floor waiting room lined with benches and chairs for the use of patients. Klima was sitting near the door of her department.

"Ruzena!" He rose and looked at her with desperate eyes. "I beg you! I beg you, be reasonable. Come with me! Let's go there together!"

His anxiety was naked, stripped of the veneer of nonchalance he had affected earlier in the week.

Ruzena said: "You just want to get rid of me."

That frightened him. "No, I don't want to get rid of you. On the contrary. I want us to be able to love each other even more."

"Stop lying to me."

"Ruzena, please! Everything will be ruined if you don't come!"

"Who says I am not coming? I still have three hours. It's only six o'clock. Go back to bed. Your wife is waiting for you."

She closed the door behind her, slipped on a white coat, and said to her middle-aged colleague: "Do me a favor. I've got to leave at nine. Could you take over for me for an hour?"

"So you let them talk you into it, after all," her friend said reproachfully.

"They didn't talk me into it. I fell in love," Ruzena replied.

4

Jakub stepped to the window and opened it. He thought of the pale blue tablet and he could not believe that the previous day he had really handed it over to that woman. He gazed at the blue sky and sucked in the brisk air of the early autumn morning. The world outside the window appeared normal, calm, matter-of-fact. The episode with the nurse now seemed to him absurd and unlikely.

He picked up the phone and dialed the bathhouse number. He asked for nurse Ruzena in the women's section. There was a long wait. At last a woman answered. He repeated that he wished to talk with nurse Ruzena. The voice replied that nurse Ruzena was now busy at the pool and could not come to the phone. He thanked her and hung up the receiver.

He felt an enormous sense of relief: Ruzena was still alive. Tablets of the kind the tube contained were generally taken three times a day: she must therefore have taken some last night and this morning, and she must have swallowed his tablet quite some time ago. Suddenly everything became quite clear to him: the pale blue pill which he had been carrying in his pocket as a guarantee of his freedom was a fake. His friend had merely given him an illusion of death.

Why hadn't he thought of that before? He recalled once again that day long ago when he had asked his friends for poison. He had just been released from prison, and now, in retrospect, he realized that his request must have appeared as a mere pose, a theatrical gesture designed to call attention to the sufferings he had undergone. Skreta had agreed without hesitation, and a few days later had brought him a shiny, pale blue pill. Yes, there was no need to hesitate, no need to try talking him out of his request: Skreta had acted wisely, much more wisely than others, who had turned down Jakub's plea. Skreta had simply given him a harmless illusion of peace and certainty, gaining Jakub's lifelong gratitude in the bargain.

How could this have failed to occur to him before? True, it did seem a little strange at the time that Skreta was giving him poison in the form of an ordinary, machine-made tablet. Jakub knew that as a biochemist Skreta had direct access to toxic substances, but it seemed peculiar that he also seemed to have tablet-making equipment at his disposal. But he had not given it much thought. Although he was skeptical about everything in this world, his faith in the pill was like faith in the Gospel.

Now, at this moment of great relief, he was of course grateful to his friend for his deception. He was happy that the nurse was alive and that the previous day's whole absurd story was only a bad dream. Nothing human lasts very long, however, and the receding waves of blissful relief were followed by a ripple of regret.

How ridiculous! The pill in his pocket had endowed his every step with dramatic pathos and had enabled him to turn his life into a noble myth! He had been convinced that the tiny piece of tissue paper had been carrying death, and instead it had contained only Skreta's silent laugh.

Jakub realized that, in the last analysis, his friend had done the right thing, but all the same it seemed to him that the Skreta he had loved suddenly shrank and became an ordinary, run-of-the-mill person, a doctor like thousands of others. The casual, unhesitating manner with which he had entrusted poison to him had made Skreta seem like an entirely different being from people of Jakub's acquaintance. He simply did not act the way other people did. There was something improbable about him. He did not seem to consider the possibility that Jakub might misuse the pill in a fit of hysteria or depression. He dealt with Jakub as if he had full confidence that he was master of himself and had no human weaknesses. They treated each other like two gods forced to live among men, and that was beautiful. That seemed unforgettable. And now it was all over.

Jakub gazed into the blue of the sky and thought: This day, Skreta gave me relief and peace. And took away my vision of himself.

5

Klima was stunned by the happy surprise of Ruzena's acquiescence, but nothing in the world could have lured him away from the waiting room. Ruzena's incomprehensible disappearance of the day before was seared into his memory. He was determined to wait right there, to make sure nobody attempted to change her mind or to carry her away.

Women patients began to come and go, drifting through the door behind which Ruzena had disappeared, some of them staying there, others returning to the waiting room to sit down in the chairs along the walls. They all looked inquisitively at Klima, for this was the women's section and men generally were not allowed in the waiting room.

A heavyset woman wearing a white coat emerged from one of the doors and gave him a searching look. She then approached him and asked if he was waiting for Ruzena. He blushed and nodded his head. "You don't have to sit around here. You've got till nine o'clock," she said with obtrusive familiarity, and it seemed to Klima that all the women in the room heard it and knew what it was about.

It was about a quarter to nine when Ruzena came out, dressed in street clothes. He took her arm and without exchanging a word they walked out of the building. They were lost in their own thoughts and neither of them noticed that Franta was following them, crouched behind the park shrubbery.

6

There was nothing left for Jakub to do except say goodbye to Olga and Skreta, but first he wanted to take a stroll through the park (for the last time) and take a last nostalgic look at the flaming trees.

He stepped out into the corridor just as a young woman was locking the door of the room opposite. Her tall figure captivated him. When he saw her face he marveled at her beauty.

"You're a friend of Dr. Skreta, aren't you?" he addressed her.

The woman smiled pleasantly. "How did you know?"

"The room you just left is the one Dr. Skreta uses for his friends," said Jakub and introduced himself.

"I am Mrs. Klima," she replied. "The doctor was good enough to give this room to my husband. I am looking for him just now. He's probably with the doctor. Do you have any idea where I might find them?"

Jakub gazed with avid pleasure at the young woman's face and it struck him (once again!) that this was his last day, which gave each event a special significance and turned it into a symbolic omen.

But what did this omen mean?

"I'll be glad to take you to Dr. Skreta," he said.

"That's very kind of you."

Yes, what did that omen mean?

First of all, it was only a message, nothing more. In two hours Jakub would be gone, and this beautiful creature would be lost to him forever. This woman revealed herself to Jakub only as a denial; he had met her only to learn that she could never be his. He had met her as an image of everything he was about to lose by his departure.

"It's strange," he said. "This is probably the last time in my life I'll ever speak to Dr. Skreta."

But the message this woman was bearing told of something else, too. It was a last-minute embassy of beauty. Yes, beauty. Jakub realized with a start that he had actually never known about beauty, that he had overlooked it and never lived for it. The beauty of this woman fascinated him. He suddenly had the feeling that all his previous decisions had been distorted because of an oversight, that he had always overlooked something. It seemed to him that if he had known this woman his decision would have been different.

"How come it's the last time?"

"I'm going abroad. For a long time."

Not that he had not had attractive women, but their charm had always been peripheral for him. What drove him toward women was thirst for revenge, or sadness and dissatisfaction, or sympathy and pity; the feminine world coincided for him with the bitter drama of life in his country, where he had been both victim and persecutor and where he had experienced many bitter struggles and few idylls. But this woman seemed removed from all that, removed from his life, she had come from outside, she had appeared out of nowhere, she had appeared not only as a beautiful woman but as beauty itself and she gave him to understand that it was possible—here and now —to live differently and for different goals, that beauty was more than justice, more than truth, more real, more certain, yes, even more attainable, that it surpassed everything else and that it was lost to him forever. She had revealed herself to him at the last moment only to make him see how foolish he had been to think that he knew everything and had tasted all that life had to offer.

"I envy you," she said.

They crossed the park together, the sky was blue, the shrubs were yellow and red, and it struck Jakub once more that this was the image of a fire consuming all the events, memories, and opportunities of his past.

"There is nothing to envy. Right now it seems to me that I should not leave at all."

"Why not? Have you suddenly found this place to your liking?"

"I have found you to my liking. I like you very, very much. You are extremely beautiful."

The words came out before he realized what was happening, and at once it occurred to him that he could tell her everything because in a few hours he would be gone and his words could have no consequences, neither for him nor for her. That suddenly discovered freedom stunned him.

"I've been living like a blind man. A blind man. Now, for the first time, I am realizing that there is such a thing as beauty. And that I have let it pass me by."

She called to Jakub's mind that realm he had never entered, the world of music and art; she seemed to merge with the burning foliage which he no longer saw as a message or symbol of fire but only as the ecstasy of beauty, awakened by the grace of her steps, the ring of her voice.

"I would do anything in the world to win you. I'd like to throw everything away and live my whole life differently, because of you and for you. But I can't, because I am really no longer here. I was supposed to leave last night, and today I'm really only here as a dallying shade."

Ah yes, now he understood why it had been given to him to have met her. This meeting was taking place outside of his life, somewhere beyond his fate, on the reverse side of his biography. That made speaking with her all the easier, until he came to realize that even so, he would never be able to tell her everything he wanted to say.

He touched her arm and pointed straight ahead: "This is where Dr. Skreta has his office. You've got to go up to the second floor."

Mrs. Klima gave him a long, searching look and Jakub drank in her gaze, soft and moist like a misty horizon. He touched her arm once more, turned, and walked off.

He glanced back and saw that Mrs. Klima was standing

motionless, looking at him. He turned several more times, and she was still there, gazing back at him.

7

_____

The waiting room was filled with about twenty nervous people. There was no room for Ruzena and Klima to sit down. The walls were decorated by large posters designed to dissuade women from undergoing abortions. *Mommy, why don't you want me?* asked a headline over a smiling baby in a crib. The lower part of the poster prominently featured a poem in which an unborn child was begging its mother not to let anyone scrape it away. The baby promised boundless happiness in return: *Whose arms will hold you when you're dying, Mommy, if you don't give me birth?*

Other posters displayed photographs of gaily laughing mothers pushing baby carriages, as well as pictures of peeing little boys. (It struck Klima that a peeing boy was an irresistible argument for childbearing. He had once seen a newsreel showing a coy little boy happily urinating, and the whole movie theater rustled with blissful female sighs.)

After waiting a while, Klima decided to knock on the examining-room door. A nurse stuck out her head, and Klima mentioned Dr. Skreta's name. The doctor appeared a few minutes later, handed Klima a form to fill out, and asked him to be patient a while longer.

Klima propped the form against the wall and began to fill out the desired information: name, date of birth, place of birth. Ruzena helped him. Then he came to the line: FATHER'S NAME. He flinched. It was terrible to see this humiliating title before him in black and white, and to sign his name to it.

Ruzena watched Klima's hand and noticed that it was trembling. That gave her great satisfaction. "Go on, write!" she said.

"Whose name should I put down?" Klima whispered.

She found him cowardly and terror-stricken, and she was full of contempt for him. He was scared of everything, scared of responsibility, even scared of signing his own name.

"What do you mean? I think it's pretty obvious whose name you should put down," she said.

"I just thought it didn't matter," said Klima.

She no longer cared for him, and deep down she was convinced that this cowardly man had injured her; it pleased her to punish him. "If you're going to turn into a liar, you and I had better part company," she said, and after he had signed his name she added with a sigh: "I'm not quite sure what I'm going to do, anyway. . . ."

"What do you mean?"

She looked at his frightened face. "Until they take it away from me, I can still change my mind."

8

She was sitting in an armchair, her legs propped up on a table, attempting to read a detective story which she had bought for the anticipated boring sojourn at the spa. But she could not concentrate on the book, because she was still thinking of the words and events of the previous evening. She was pleased with everything that had happened, and she was especially pleased with herself. At last she had turned into the person she had always wanted to be: not the victim of masculine desires, but the creator of her own history. She had totally discarded the role of innocent ward, assigned to her by Jakub; on the contrary, she had transformed Jakub in accord with her own wishes.

She now thought of herself as elegant, independent, and daring. She contemplated her legs stretched out on the table, encased in tight jeans, and when she heard a knock on the door she answered breezily: "Come in, I've been waiting for you!"

Jakub entered, looking unhappy.

"Hello!" she said, taking her time before shifting her legs. Jakub seemed flustered, and that pleased her. She rose and kissed him lightly on the cheek. "Will you stay a while?"

"No," answered Jakub in a sad voice. "This time it's really goodbye. I'm leaving in a short while. I thought I'd walk you over to the baths for the last time."

"Fine," said Olga with a cheerful smile, "I'd enjoy a little stroll."

9

Jakub was filled to overflowing with the image of the beautiful Mrs. Klima. The night with Olga had left him uneasy and confused, and he had had to overcome a certain distaste to come and bid her farewell. But he would not reveal these feelings for anything in the world. He told himself that he needed to behave with extraordinary tact, and that she must not have the slightest inkling how little pleasure and joy he had found in her lovemaking. Nothing must be allowed to spoil her memory of him. He put on a serious face, couched the most trivial of sentences in a melancholy tone, kept on touching her arm, stroking her hair, and whenever she looked him in the eye he tried to put on as downcast an expression as possible.

She suggested that they might have time to stop somewhere for a few glasses of wine, but Jakub wanted to make their farewell as brief as possible because he was finding the experience wearing. "Saying goodbye is so sad. I don't want to prolong it," he said.

When they reached the entrance to the baths he reached for both of her hands and gazed deep into her eyes.

Olga said: "It was awfully good of you to come and see me, Jakub. Last night was beautiful. I am glad that you finally stopped acting like my daddy and turned into Jakub. It was really terrific. Wasn't it terrific?"

Jakub understood that he understood nothing. Was it possible that this sensitive girl considered last night's lovemaking mere entertainment? That she was motivated by mere sensuality, with no feelings? That the pleasant memory of one night of love outweighed the sorrow of lifelong separation?

He kissed her. She wished him a happy journey and turned toward the broad portals of the baths.

10)

He had been pacing back and forth in front of the clinic for almost two hours, and he was becoming impatient. He continually reminded himself that he must not create a scene, but he felt that his powers of self-control were nearing an end.

He entered the building. The spa was a small place and everyone knew him. He asked the doorman if he had seen Ruzena. The doorman nodded and said that she had gone up in the elevator. The elevator stopped only on the top floor, the fourth, and the lower two floors were reached by a stairway. Franta could thus narrow his search to the corridors on the fourth floor. On one side were offices, and the other side was taken up by a gynecology clinic. He walked down the first corridor (where he could not find a living soul), and then investigated the second one, with the unpleasant feeling that men were not welcome here. He saw a nurse whose face looked familiar and asked her about Ruzena. She pointed to a door at the end of the hall. It was open, and several men and women clustered around it. Franta went in, saw several more women sitting inside, but the trumpeter and Ruzena were not there.

"Did you by any chance see a young lady, kind of a blond young lady?"

A woman pointed toward the office door: "They're inside."

Mommy, why don't you want me? read Franta, and saw the other posters with pictures of grinning infants and urinating boys. It was all becoming very clear to him.

11

The middle of the room was taken up by a long table. Klima and Ruzena were sitting on one side, and facing them was Dr. Skreta, bracketed by a pair of hefty, middle-aged ladies.

Dr. Skreta glanced at the applicants and shook his head in a gesture of disapproval. "It makes me sick at heart to look at you. Do you have any idea how much trouble we take, trying to restore fertility to women who want to have babies? And here you are— young, healthy, mature people—and you voluntarily want to give up the most precious thing in life. I want to make it quite clear that the purpose of this commission is not to encourage abortions but to regulate them."

The two portly matrons murmured approval and Dr. Skreta resumed his admonishment of the applicants. Klima's heart was pounding. He guessed that Dr. Skreta's remarks were not intended for him but for the benefit of the two fellow members of the commission, who hated abortion-seeking young women with all the majestic power of their maternal bellies. But Klima was terrified lest those words soften Ruzena's resolve. Had she not hinted a few minutes earlier that her mind was not yet made up?

"What do you want to live for?" continued Dr. Skreta. "Life without children is like a tree without leaves. If I had the authority I would prohibit abortion altogether. Aren't you two concerned that our population rate is going down year by year? And yet no country in the world takes better care of its mothers and babies! In no country in the world is a newborn infant assured of a more secure future!"

Once again the two commission members mumbled approvingly and Dr. Skreta went on: "Our friend here is married and is now worried about assuming all the consequences of irresponsible sexual conduct. But you should have thought of that before, comrade!"

Dr. Skreta was silent for a few moments, and then turned once more to Klima. "You have no children. Now tell me honestly: Is it really out of the question for you to divorce your wife, for the sake of this unborn child?"

"It's impossible," replied Klima.

"I know, I know." Dr. Skreta sighed. "I have received a psychiatric report to the effect that Mrs. Klima is suffering from suicidal tendencies. The birth of this child would endanger one person's life, destroy a marriage, and create one more unwed mother. What can we do?" He sighed once more, then picked up a pen and signed the form, and pushed it toward the two matrons, who also sighed and signed their names at the bottom.

"The procedure will be performed on Monday of next week at eight in the morning," Dr. Skreta declared, and motioned to Ruzena that she was free to leave.

One of the portly ladies turned to Klima. "You stay here a moment." After Ruzena left, she continued: "An abortion is not such a simple thing as you imagine. It involves a great loss of blood. Through your irresponsibility you will have robbed comrade Ruzena of her blood, and it is only fair that you pay it back." She pushed some sort of form before Klima and said: "Sign here."

The bewildered trumpeter obeyed.

"That is an application for voluntary blood donation. You can go next door and the nurse will take your blood right now."

12

Ruzena quickly passed through the waiting room with downcast eyes and did not see Franta until he shouted at her in the corridor:

"What were you doing there?"

She was frightened by his furious looks and walked faster.

"I am asking you what you were doing there."

"None of your business."

"I know what you were doing!"

"If you know then don't ask."

They were descending the stairs and Ruzena was hurrying, wanting to get away from Franta and from the conversation.

"That was the abortion commission. I know it. And you want them to take the baby away!"

"I'll do as I please."

"You won't do as you please! I am involved, too."

Ruzena was rushing, almost running, with Franta right behind her. When they reached the gate to the bathhouse, she said: "Don't you dare follow me. I'm working. Don't bother me now."

Franta was excited: "Don't you tell me what to do!"

"You have no right to bother me!"

"And you have no right to shut me out!"

Ruzena dashed into the building, with Franta close on her heels.

13

Jakub was glad that it was all over and there was only one thing left for him to do: say goodbye to Skreta. Slowly, he set out across the park to Marx House.

From the opposite direction, along the broad park promenade, came a group of about twenty schoolchildren led by their teacher. She had the end of a red string in her hand, and the children marched along single file, holding on to the string. They were walking slowly, and the teacher was pointing out to them various trees and shrubs. Jakub stopped, because he had never studied natural science and could never remember that an alder was an alder and a hornbeam a hornbeam.

"This is a linden," the teacher said, pointing at a bushy, yellowing tree.

Jakub examined the children. They all wore blue coats and red caps. They looked like little brothers and sisters. He scrutinized their faces and it seemed to him that they resembled one another not only in dress but in features as well. At least seven of them had markedly large noses and broad mouths. They looked like Dr. Skreta.

He recalled the big-nosed child of the innkeeper. Was it possible that Skreta's eugenics dream was more than a fantasy? That this region was really being populated by the Great Father Skreta?

Jakub found the idea absurd. All these children looked alike because all children in the world look alike.

But then the idea recurred: Suppose Skreta was really turning his strange plan into reality? What was to prevent such a bizarre scheme from being realized?

"And that tree over there, what do we call that one?"

"That's a birch!" answered a little Skreta. Yes, it was Skreta through and through; he not only had a big nose, but wore glasses and had the nasal voice that made the speech of Jakub's friend so touchingly comical.

"Correct, Olda!" said the teacher.

It occurred to Jakub that in ten or twenty years the country would be inhabited by thousands of Skretas. Once again he was overwhelmed by the peculiar feeling that he had been living in his own homeland without having had any real notion what was going on. He had been living, as they say, in the center of the action. He had taken part in current events. He had dabbled in politics, and it had virtually cost him his life. Even after they had pushed him out, he had kept up with political developments. He had always thought that he was listening to the heartbeat of his country. And yet what did he really hear? A nation's pulse? Perhaps it was only an old alarm clock, an obsolete old clock which measured the wrong time. Had all those political struggles been but a delusion which distracted him from the really important things in life?

The teacher led her young charges further down the park lane and Jakub still could not get the image of the beautiful woman out of his mind. The recollection of her beauty continued to torment him with recurrent questions: Had he been living in a world entirely different from what he supposed? Had he been seeing everything topsy-turvy? Suppose beauty meant more than truth, suppose it had really been an angel that had presented Bartleff with a dahlia flower?

"And what is that?" He heard the teacher's voice.

"A maple," answered a miniature, bespectacled Skreta.

14

Ruzena ran up the stairway, trying not to look back over her shoulder. She slammed the door to her department behind her and hurried to the dressing room, slipped the white nurse's coat over her bare body, and let out a deep sigh of relief. The unpleasantness with Franta had disturbed her, yet in some strange way it had purged her of anxiety. Both of them, Franta and Klima, now seemed distant and unfamiliar.

She stepped into the hall lined with beds where women patients were resting after their baths. Her middle-aged colleague was sitting at a table near the door. "Did they approve it?" she asked coolly.

"Yes. Thanks for taking over," said Ruzena and proceeded to furnish the next patient with her locker key and fresh sheet.

No sooner had the older nurse left than the door opened and Franta's head appeared.

"It's not true that it's none of my business! It concerns both of us. I've got something to say, too!"

"Get lost!" she hissed at him. "This is the women's section! Get lost this minute or I'll have you thrown out!"

Franta was flushed with anger and Ruzena's threat infuriated him so much that he barged into the room and slammed the door. "I don't give a damn what you do! I don't give a damn!" he shouted.

"I'm telling you to get out of here at once!" said Ruzena.

"I see right through you! It's all the fault of that bastard!

That bugler! It's all just a farce anyway, just a question of pull! He fixed it with that doctor, they're big jazz buddies! But I see through the whole thing and I won't let you murder my child! I am the father and I have something to say! And I forbid you to murder my child!"

Franta was shouting and the patients were stirring under their blankets and lifting their heads with curiosity.

Ruzena too was getting excited, because Franta seemed to be getting out of control and she did not know how to manage the situation.

"It's not your baby at all," she said. "I don't know how you got that idea. It's not yours at all."

"What?" yelled Franta, and advanced further into the room, sidestepping the table and coming face to face with Ruzena. "Not my baby? What the hell do you mean? I know damn well it's mine!"

At this moment a woman walked in from the pool, naked and dripping wet, and Ruzena was supposed to dry her and put her to bed. The patient was startled to come upon Franta, who was standing just a few steps away from her, gazing at her with unseeing eyes.

For the moment, Ruzena was saved. She skipped over to the woman, threw a sheet over her, and led her to the bed.

"What's that man doing here?" the patient asked, glancing back at Franta.

"He's a madman! He is stark raving mad and I don't know how to get him out of here. I just don't know what to do with him," said Ruzena, wrapping the patient in a warm blanket.

"Hey, mister!" another resting woman called out. "You've got no business here! Get out!"

"I do so have business here," Franta retorted stubbornly and refused to budge. When Ruzena returned he was no longer flushed but pale. He spoke softly, resolutely: "I'll tell you something: If you let them take that baby, they can bury me at the same time. If you murder that child you'll have two lives on your conscience."

Ruzena sighed and opened the drawer of her table. It contained her handbag with the tube of pale blue pills. She shook one of them into her palm and popped it into her mouth.

Franta was no longer shouting but pleading: "I beg you, Ruzena. I beg you. I can't live without you. I'll kill myself."

At that moment Ruzena felt a sharp stab of pain in her stomach and Franta watched her face distort with agony, become unrecognizable, her eyes staring, unseeing; he saw her doubling over, pressing her hands to her belly, slumping to the floor.

15

Olga was splashing around in the pool when she suddenly heard . . . What did she actually hear? It was hard to say. The hall had suddenly become full of confusion. The women around her were climbing out of the pool and pressing into the adjoining room, which seemed to have turned into a vortex sucking up everything around it. Olga, too, found herself caught up in this irresistible pull, and without thinking, led only by anxious curiosity, she followed the others.

Near the door she saw a group of women. They had their backs to her, naked and wet, bending over with their behinds stuck in the air. She saw a young man standing to one side.

More naked women came pressing into the room and as Olga approached closer she saw nurse Ruzena lying motionless on the floor. The young man suddenly dropped to his knees next to her and shouted: "I killed her! It's me! I am the murderer!"

The women were dripping wet. One of them leaned over the prone body of Ruzena and tried to feel her pulse. But it was a useless gesture, for the nurse was dead and nobody had any doubt about it. The bare, wet bodies of the women impatiently pressed forward in order to get an intimate glimpse of death, to see its presence on a familiar face.

Franta was still kneeling on the floor. He threw his arms around Ruzena and kissed her face.

The women were looming over him. Franta glanced up at

them and repeated: "I killed her! Arrest me!"

One of the women said: "Let's do something!" and another ran out into the hall and began shouting for help. Soon two of Ruzena's colleagues came running, followed by a doctor in a white coat.

Only then did it occur to Olga that she was naked, that she was pushing and shoving amid other naked women, in front of two male strangers, a young man and a doctor. She realized the absurdity of the situation. But Olga also knew that this realization was not about to change anything, that she would continue to shove and elbow a while longer in order to gaze on death, which fascinated and attracted her.

The doctor was holding Ruzena's wrist in a vain attempt to feel her pulse, while Franta kept repeating: "I killed her. Call the police. Arrest me."

10

Jakub caught up with his friend just as he got back to his office from the clinic. He praised Skreta's performance on the drums and excused himself for not having waited after the concert.

"I'm sorry you left so soon," Dr. Skreta said. "Yesterday was your last full day here and God knows where you've been keeping yourself. We had so many things to discuss. And the worst of it is that you probably spent your time with that skinny girl. Gratitude is a dangerous emotion."

"What do you mean, gratitude? Why should I be grateful to her?"

"You wrote me that her father had been kind to you."

That day Dr. Skreta had no office hours and the gynecologic-examination table loomed deserted in the back of the room. The two friends made themselves comfortable in a pair of armchairs.

"No, gratitude had nothing to do with it," Jakub resumed.

"I wanted you to take her under your wing and the simplest thing that came to my mind was to say that I was obligated to her father. But actually the truth is quite different. I am now ringing down the curtain on that part of my life, so I might as well tell you the true story. I was sent to prison with the full approval of her father. In fact, her father actually thought he was sending me to my death. Six months later he was executed himself, while I was lucky and saved my neck."

"In other words, she is the daughter of a scoundrel," Dr. Skreta said.

Jakub shrugged. "He believed that I was an enemy of the revolution. Everyone was saying that about me, and he believed it."

"So why did you tell me he was your friend?"

"We were friends once. That's why he was so proud of having cast his vote to condemn me. This proved that he placed ideals above friendship. At the moment he branded me a traitor to the revolution, he thought that he was subordinating his personal interests for something higher, and he thought of it as the greatest act of his life."

"And that's the reason you like that homely girl?"

"She had nothing to do with it. She is innocent."

"There are thousands of other innocent girls. If you picked out that particular one it was probably because she was her father's daughter."

Jakub shrugged his shoulders, and Dr. Skreta continued: "There is the same perverted streak in you as in him. It seems to me that you, too, consider your friendship with this girl as the greatest act of your life. You denied your natural hatred, you suppressed your natural distaste, just to prove to yourself how noble you are. It's touching, but it's also unnatural and totally unnecessary."

"You're wrong," Jakub countered. "I didn't want to suppress anything and I had no illusion about being noble. I simply felt sorry for her. As soon as I set eyes on her. She was still a child when she was driven from her native town, she lived with her mother in some mountain village where the people were afraid to have anything to do with them. For a long time she was kept from studying, even though she is a gifted girl. It is terrible to persecute children for their parents' politics. Was I, too, supposed to hate her because of her father? I felt pity for her. I was sorry for her because they had killed her father, and I was sorry for her because her father had found it necessary to send a comrade to his death."

The telephone rang. Skreta lifted the receiver and listened. He looked irritated and said: "I'm quite busy right now. Do you really need me?" After another pause he said: "Oh, all right then. I am coming." He hung up and muttered a curse.

"If you've got something to do, don't let me keep you, I've got to be leaving anyway," said Jakub, rising from his chair.

"Damn it," said Skreta. "We didn't get a chance to talk about anything. There was something I wanted to discuss with you today. Now I have lost the thread. It was something very important, too. I've been thinking about it since morning. Do you have any idea what it might have been?"

"No," said Jakub.

"Damn it. And now they want me at the baths. . . ."

"This is the best way to say goodbye. Right in the middle of a conversation," Jakub said, and squeezed his friend's hand.

17

Ruzena's dead body was lying in a small room normally reserved for doctors on night duty. Several people were shuffling around the room. A police inspector had already arrived, too, interrogated Franta, and written down his statement. Franta once more pleaded to be arrested.

"Did you give her the pill?" asked the inspector.

"No."

"Then stop saying you killed her."

"She always threatened to kill herself," Franta said.

"Why?"

"She said she'd kill herself if I didn't stop bothering her. She said she didn't want a baby, and that rather than have a baby she'd kill herself first."

Dr. Skreta entered. He exchanged a friendly greeting with the inspector and stepped up to the dead girl; he lifted her eyelid and examined the conjunctiva.

"Doctor, you were this nurse's superior?" the inspector asked.

"Yes."

"Do you think she may have used a poison available in your practice?"

Skreta inquired about the details of Ruzena's death. Then he said: "It doesn't sound like any drug she could have gotten in our office. It must have been some sort of alkaloid. As to which one, that will have to be determined by autopsy."

"How could she have obtained such a drug?"

"Alkaloids are substances derived from certain plants. I have no idea how she could have obtained an alkaloid preparation."

"Everything seems very mysterious," the inspector said. "Even the motive. This young man stated that she was pregnant with his child and that she was planning to undergo an abortion."

"He made her do it!" shouted Franta.

"Who?" the inspector asked.

"That trumpeter! He wanted to take her away from me, and he forced her to have my baby removed! I checked up on them. They applied to the abortion commission!"

"I can confirm that," Dr. Skreta said. "Today we indeed discussed this nurse's request for abortion."

"And the musician was with her?" the inspector asked.

"Yes," Skreta said. "Nurse Ruzena named him as the father of her child."

"It's a lie! The child is mine!" Franta shouted.

"Nobody doubts that," Dr. Skreta said, "but nurse Ruzena

had to name as father someone who was already married, so that the commission would approve the abortion."

"So you knew all along that it was a dirty lie!" Franta shouted at Dr. Skreta.

"According to the law, the woman has the decisive word. Ruzena told us that she was carrying Klima's child, Klima concurred, so none of us had the right to challenge her statement."

"But you did not believe the claim of Mr. Klima's paternity?" asked the inspector.

"No."

"What led you to this opinion?"

"Altogether, Mr. Klima visited our spa only twice, and each time his visit was very short. It is highly unlikely that any intimate contact ever took place between him and Ruzena. Our spa is too small for such news to remain secret for very long. Most likely, Mr. Klima's alleged paternity was just camouflage, and nurse Ruzena persuaded Mr. Klima to go along with it so that the commission would give its approval for an abortion. As you can guess, this fellow right here would hardly have been as cooperative."

Franta was no longer following Skreta's talk. His mind had gone blank. He only kept hearing Ruzena's words: *You'll drive me to suicide, you'll drive me to it for sure.* He was convinced that he had caused her death, and yet he could not quite understand why, and he could not make any sense out of it all. He was standing like a savage face to face with a miracle, like a man stunned by an enigma, he had become deaf and dumb because his senses were unable to grasp the unfathomable.

(Poor Franta, you will walk through your life without understanding, you will only know that your love killed a woman you loved, you will walk with a secret sign of doom on your forehead, an uncomprehending Cain, a courier of disaster.)

He was pale, as inert as a pillar of salt. He did not notice that a man had excitedly entered the room, approached the dead girl, gazed at her for a long time, and stroked her hair.

Dr. Skreta whispered: "Suicide. Poison."

The newly arrived man turned his head sharply. "Suicide? I know with all my heart and soul that this woman did not take her life. If she swallowed poison it must have been murder."

The inspector looked at the man in astonishment. It was Bartleff, and his eyes were burning with angry fire.

18

Jakub turned the ignition key and drove off. Soon he had passed the last villas of the spa and found himself in open country. The border was about four hours away, and he had no wish to hurry. The knowledge that he would never see this country again made the land take on a precious quality. It seemed to him that he did not recognize it, that it looked different from the way he remembered it, and that it was a pity he could not stay longer.

And yet he realized that postponing his departure, whether by one day or one year, would not really change anything. He would not get to know the country any more intimately, no matter how long he stayed. He must make peace with the sad truth that he was leaving his homeland without having gotten to know it, without having profited from all it had to offer, that he was a debtor who had not paid his obligations as well as a creditor who had failed to collect his due.

Then he thought of the girl to whom he had given sham poison and he told himself that his career as murderer was the shortest of his life. He smiled: I was a murderer for eighteen hours.

But then he mentally retorted: No, it was not true that he had been a murderer for but a brief time—he was a murderer still, and would remain one for the rest of his life. For it was not important whether the pale blue pill contained real poison or not; what mattered was that he had been convinced of its lethal power and yet had handed it to a stranger without making any real attempt to save her.

He reflected about it with the equanimity of a man who believes that his actions have been mere experiments without consequences in the real world.

His act of murder was a strange one: murder without a motive. Nothing was to be gained by it. Then what sense did it make? Clearly, its only sense was to make him see that he was a murderer.

Murder as experiment, as an act of self-revelation, this was a familiar story: the story of Raskolnikov. He murdered in order to answer for himself the question: Does a man have the right to kill an inferior human being, and would he be strong enough to bear the consequences? The murder was a question posed to his own self.

Yes, there was something about Jakub's act that related him to Raskolnikov: the meaninglessness of the murder, its theoretical quality. But there were differences, too: Raskolnikov was asking whether an outstanding person had the right to sacrifice an inferior existence for the sake of his own advantage. But when Jakub had handed the tube to the nurse, he had had nothing like that in mind. Jakub was not interested in exploring the question of whether one person had the right to sacrifice the life of another. On the contrary, Jakub was convinced that nobody had such a right. In fact, the ease with which various men and women arrogated this right to themselves terrified him. Jakub was living in a world where human lives were readily being destroyed for the sake of abstract ideas. He knew the faces of those arrogant men and women: not evil but virtuous, burning with righteous zeal or shining with jovial comradeship; faces reflecting militant innocence. Still others were marked by pious cowardice, murmuring excuses yet diligently carrying out sentences they all knew to be cruel and unjust. Jakub knew those faces and hated them. In addition, Jakub knew that all human beings secretly wish for someone's death, and only two things prevent them from acting out their wish: fear of punishment and the physical difficulties of committing murder. Jakub knew that if every person on earth had the power to murder secretly and at long range, humanity would die out within a few minutes. He therefore considered Raskolnikov's experiment totally unnecessary.

Then why had he handed the nurse that poison? Had it perhaps been just an accident? After all, Raskolnikov had spent a long time thinking about his plan and preparing for it, whereas he had acted on the impulse of a mere moment. And yet Jakub realized that he, too, had unknowingly been preparing for many years and that the instant in which he handed the poison to Ruzena became like a crevice where all his past life, all his disgust with people, could be lodged and gain leverage.

Raskolnikov, about to commit the ax murder of the old money lender, realized that he was on the edge of a terrible threshold; that he was on the verge of transgressing God's commandment; that even though the old woman was a wretched creature, she was nevertheless a creature of God. Jakub did not feel such Raskolnikovian fear. For him, people were not creatures of God. Jakub loved nobility and refinement, but he had learned that these were not human qualities. He knew people well, and for that reason did not like them. Jakub was noble, and thus gave them poison.

I am a murderer through nobility of soul, he said to himself, and it seemed comical and sad.

Raskolnikov, after killing the old money lender, was not able to control the fearsome storm of reproach that burst in his conscience. Jakub, deeply convinced that a human being had no right to sacrifice the lives of others, felt no pangs of remorse at all. And yet the nurse whom he had poisoned was surely a more likable being that Raskolnikov's usurious hag.

He tried to test himself by pretending that the nurse was really dead. No, this idea failed to fill him with any sense of guilt, and Jakub drove calmly and peacefully through the pleasant countryside which was saying its gentle farewell.

Raskolnikov experienced his act of murder as a tragedy, and staggered under the weight of his deed. Jakub was amazed to find that his deed was weightless, easy to bear, light as air. And he wondered whether there was not more horror in this lightness than in all the dark agonies and contortions of the Russian hero.

He drove slowly, interrupting his thoughts now and again by gazing at the landscape. He told himself that the episode of the pill had only been a game, a game without consequences, typical of his whole life, which had left no traces, no roots, no mark in this land —a land he was now leaving like a puff of wind.

19

Lighter by a quarter of a liter of blood, Klima was impatiently waiting for Dr. Skreta in his waiting room. He did not wish to leave the spa without saying goodbye to the doctor and without asking him to look after Ruzena. *Until they actually take it away from me, I can still change my mind*—these words of Ruzena's still rang in his ears and terrified him. He was afraid that once he left and Ruzena was no longer under his influence she might change her mind at the last minute.

Dr. Skreta appeared at last. Klima rushed to shake his hand, to say goodbye, and to thank him for the wonderful job he had done on the drums.

"It was a beautiful evening," Dr. Skreta said, "you were great. There is nothing I'd rather do than have another concert just like it. Maybe we can arrange performances at other spas."

"I'd love to, I really enjoyed the way you backed me up!" the trumpeter said with warmth, adding: "There is one favor I want to ask of you: please keep your eye on Ruzena. I'm afraid that some foolish idea might creep into her head. Women are so unpredictable."

"Nothing will creep into her head anymore, don't worry," Dr. Skreta said. "Ruzena is dead."

Klima did not quite grasp Skreta's meaning, and the doctor

had to explain what had happened. Then he said: "It is suicide, but it looks somewhat mysterious. People could get all sorts of funny ideas—you know, killing herself one hour after appearing before the abortion commission. But please don't worry." He grasped the trumpeter by the arm when he saw him turning pale. "Fortunately, that nurse of ours had an affair with a young mechanic who is convinced that the child is his. I declared that you never had any intimacy with Ruzena and that she had talked you into playing the father because the commission rules out abortion when both members of the couple are unmarried. I just want you to be prepared, in case they ask you any questions. I see that your nerves are in bad shape and that's a pity. You've got to pull yourself together, there are lots of concerts ahead of us!"

Completely at a loss for words, Klima just kept on squeezing Dr. Skreta's hand.

Kamila was waiting for him in his room at Richmond House. Klima pressed her close and then began kissing her fervently—first all over her face, then he kneeled in front of her and kissed her dress down to the hem.

"What's come over you?"

"Nothing. I am just so happy to be with you. I'm so happy you exist."

They packed their luggage and carried it to the car. He said he was tired and asked her to take the wheel.

They drove in silence. Klima was exhausted, yet enormously relieved. The idea that he might be questioned made him somewhat uneasy. He feared that Kamila could learn something that way. But he repeated to himself Dr. Skreta's words. Even if he were to be interrogated, he would assume the innocent (and in his country not uncommon) role of a gentleman who pretended paternity just to do a young lady a favor. Nobody could blame him for such a chivalrous act, not even Kamila.

He looked at her. Her beauty filled the small space of the car like a heady perfume. He felt he would be happy and content to breathe that perfume for the rest of his days. In his mind he heard the soft, distant sound of a trumpet and he resolved that for the rest of his life he would make music only to please this woman, his precious darling, his one and only love.

20

Whenever she sat behind the wheel, she felt at once stronger and more independent. But this time it was not only the role of driver that gave her self-confidence, but also the words of the stranger she had met in the hall of Richmond House. She could not get those words out of her mind. Nor could she forget his face, so much more virile than the smooth cheeks of her husband. It struck Kamila that she had actually never known a real man.

Out of the corner of her eye she glanced at the trumpeter's tired visage, which seemed to have sagged into an enigmatically contented smile while his hand was stroking her shoulder.

This excess of tenderness neither pleased nor moved her. Its puzzling motivation only confirmed her suspicion that the trumpeter was keeping some secret from her, that he was leading some hidden, separate existence from which he was excluding her. This time, however, she did not react with anguish but only with indifference.

What had that man said? That he was leaving forever. Her heart was sad with a soft, lingering yearning. Not only a yearning for this man, but for lost opportunity, not only this one but opportunity in general. She mourned for all the opportunities she had wasted, missed, brushed aside, even for those she had never known at all.

The stranger had said that he had been living like a blind man and that he had never realized there was such a thing as beauty. She understood him. Was it not the same with her? She, too, had lived in blindness. She had eyes for only a single figure, lit up by the powerful beam of jealousy. What if that searchlight were suddenly to be turned off? Thousands of other figures would come forth into the light of day, and the man who had seemed unique in the world would simply turn into one of many.

She was holding the wheel, she felt self-confident and beautiful, and it occurred to her: Was it really love that bound her to Klima —or only the fear of losing him? And even if at the beginning that fear had been an anxious form of love, had not love (overworked and exhausted) faded, leaving but an empty form? Perhaps all she had left was fear itself, fear without love? And what would remain if she ever lost that fear?

At her side, the trumpeter was again smiling for no apparent reason. She glanced at him and told herself that once she lost her jealousy, nothing would be left at all. She was hurtling forward, and suddenly she knew that somewhere ahead there was a parting of the ways. For the first time since her marriage to the trumpeter, the idea of parting from him produced no anxiety whatever.

21

Olga entered Bartleff's apartment and excused herself: "Please don't be angry with me for barging in like this. But I am in such a nervous state that I can't stand being alone. Are you sure I am not disturbing you?"

The police inspector was also in the room, along with Bartleff and Skreta. He answered: "No, you are not disturbing us. We're through with official business and are just chatting."

"The inspector is an old friend of mine," Dr. Skreta explained to Olga.

"Why in the world did she do it?"

"She had a fight with her boyfriend. In the middle of the argument she suddenly pulled something out of her handbag and stuck it in her mouth. That's all we know, and I'm afraid that's all we'll ever know."

"Inspector, please," Bartleff said insistently, "I urge you to bear in mind what I told you in my statement. Ruzena spent her last night with me in this very room. Maybe I didn't make the point clear enough to you: It was a wonderful night, and Ruzena was extremely happy. This plain, ordinary girl only needed to throw off the shackles of her unfriendly and apathetic environment to become an entirely different being—a radiant being full of love, tenderness, nobility. You have no notion what a fine person was locked inside of her. I repeat: Last night I opened a door for her to a new kind of life, and she was thirsting to start living it. But someone crossed my path." Bartleff paused, then added softly: "It must have been the powers of hell."

"When it comes to the powers of darkness, I'm afraid the police have no jurisdiction," the inspector said.

Bartleff ignored the ironic remark. "A verdict of suicide would be absolute nonsense in this case, please try to understand that! She couldn't possibly have killed herself just as she was beginning to live! I tell you once again that I will not permit anyone to accuse her of suicide."

"My dear sir," the inspector replied, "nobody is accusing her of suicide. For one thing, suicide is not a crime. It has nothing to do with criminal justice. It's not our concern."

"Yes," said Bartleff, "you don't consider suicide a crime because for you life simply means existence. But for me, inspector, there is no greater sin than suicide. It's worse than murder. Murder can be motivated by revenge or greed, but even greed is a kind of perverse love of life. But someone who kills himself throws God's gift into the dust with a mocking laugh. Suicide is spitting in the face of the Creator. I tell you that I will do everything I can to prove that this girl was innocent. You say she killed herself. But tell me why. What possible motive could she have had?"

"The motives for suicide are always something of a mystery," the inspector said. "And besides, it's not my job to look for them. You mustn't be angry with me for sticking strictly to my duties. I have plenty of them and I have barely enough time as it is. The case is not closed, but I can tell you right now that I don't expect any dramatic new developments."

"You surprise me, inspector," said Bartleff in an extremely icy tone. "I'm surprised at how quickly you're ready to put a period to the story of a human life."

Olga noticed that the inspector's face flushed with anger. But then he controlled himself, and after a short pause said in a voice that was almost too gentle: "All right then. Let's assume that you're right and a murder has taken place. Let's try to imagine how it might have happened. In the handbag of the deceased we found a tube of sedatives. Let's assume that Ruzena wanted to take one of the pills in the tube, but someone had substituted a different pill which looked similar but contained poison."

"You think that the poison which Ruzena swallowed came out of the tube of sedatives?" asked Dr. Skreta.

"Of course, the poison might have been lying in the handbag separately. That would have been the case if there was a suicide. But if we assume that we're dealing with murder, then there is only one possibility: somebody had put a poisoned pill into the tube, a pill with the same shape and color as the sedative."

"I beg to differ," Dr. Skreta said. "It isn't so easy to turn an alkaloid into a smoothly shaped tablet. It could only have been made by somebody with access to a tableting machine. And nobody around here is in such a position."

"Are you saying that it would have been impossible for anyone in this vicinity to have prepared such a pill?"

"Not impossible. But extremely difficult."

"For my purposes, it is sufficient that such a possibility existed," said the inspector, continuing: "Now let's examine the question as to who might have had any interest in seeing this girl dead. She was not wealthy, so we can rule out greed. We can also eliminate political motives or espionage. We are left with motives of an intimate nature. Now who are our likely suspects? First of all her lover, who had a heated quarrel with her just before she died. Do you think that he slipped her the poison?"

Nobody answered the inspector's question, and he continued: "I don't believe so. That boy was still fighting to keep the girl. He wanted to marry her. She was pregnant with his child, and even if the child was someone else's, the important thing was that he was convinced he was the father. The moment he found out she wanted an abortion he became desperate. But please bear in mind that Ruzena was coming back from a hearing, not from an actual abortion! As far as our desperate hero was concerned, all was not yet lost. The fetus was still alive within her body and he was ready to do anything to save it. It would be absurd to think that he poisoned her, when he was so eager to be her husband and the father of her child. Besides, Dr. Skreta just explained to us that it is not easy for the average person to get hold of poison shaped like an ordinary pill. How would this fellow manage to get such a thing, a naïve boy without social contacts? Can anyone explain that to me?"

Bartleff, to whom the inspector kept turning, shrugged his shoulders.

"All right then. Let's consider other suspects. There is the trumpet player from the city. He had made the acquaintance of the deceased several months ago. We don't know how intimate they became, and we'll never know. In any case, he became sufficiently friendly with the deceased that she felt free to ask him to assume paternity of the child and to accompany her before the abortion commission. Why did she ask him rather than some local man? That's easy to guess. Any married man living in this area would have been afraid of gossip and trouble at home. Only somebody who lived in a distant locality could have performed this service for her. Besides, the rumor that she was pregnant with the child of a famous artist was flattering to the nurse, and could not possibly harm the trumpeter's reputation. We can therefore assume that Mr. Klima did not hesitate to perform this favor. Then why kill the poor nurse? As Dr. Skreta told us earlier, it is highly unlikely that Mr. Klima actually was the father of the unborn child. But for the sake of argument let's examine even that possibility. Let's assume that Klima was the father, and that this was highly unpleasant to him. But tell me, why in the world would he murder her when she had agreed to submit to an abortion and this step had been officially approved? What possible reason could we have, Mr. Bartleff, to regard Klima as a murderer?"

"You don't understand me," Bartleff replied softly. "I'm not interested in sending anyone to the gallows. I only wish to exonerate Ruzena. Because suicide is the most grievous of sins. Even the most cruel suffering may have mysterious value, and even life on the edge of death can be beautiful. A person who has not looked death in the face does not know this, but I know it, inspector. And that is why I insist that I will do everything in my power to prove that this girl was innocent."

"I share your concern, believe me," said the inspector. "After all, there is a third suspect to be considered. Mr. Bartleff: American businessman. As he himself admitted, the deceased spent her last night with him. It might be objected that a murderer would hardly volunteer such information. But this objection is not valid. Mr. Bartleff sat next to Ruzena at a crowded concert, and everyone clearly saw the two of them leaving together. Mr. Bartleff may well realize that in such a situation he would be better off volunteering the obvious truth himself. Mr. Bartleff tells us that this was an extremely happy night for Ruzena. And why not? Mr. Bartleff is not only a fascinating man, but he is above all an American businessman with lots of dollars and an American passport which enables him to travel all over the world. Ruzena was stuck in this small place, desperately looking for a way out. She had a boyfriend who wanted to marry her, but he was an unsophisticated local mechanic. If she were to marry him she would seal her fate forever and could never hope to escape from here. She had nobody else so she stayed with him. But she resisted binding herself to him irrevocably because she did not want to give up all hope of a different kind of life. And then suddenly a worldly, gallant man appeared on the scene who completely turned her head. She dreamed that he would marry her and take her away to a distant land. A discreet mistress at first, she gradually became more and more demanding. She made it clear that she would never give him up and began to blackmail him. Bartleff is married and I understand that his wife is due to arrive tomorrow from America. As far as I know, he loves his wife, the mother of his infant child. Bartleff was ready to do anything to avoid a scandal. He knew that Ruzena was in the habit of carrying a tube of sedatives, and he knew what they looked like. He was a wealthy man with extensive contacts abroad. It was easy for him to have somebody manufacture a poison pill in the shape of Ruzena's sedatives. In the course of that beautiful night, while his beloved was asleep, he secretly inserted the poisonous pill in the tube. It is my belief, Mr. Bartleff," the inspector dramatically raised his voice, "that you are the only person who had the motive and the means to murder nurse Ruzena. I call upon you to confess."

The room was quiet. The inspector looked straight at Bartleff, who returned his gaze with equal calmness. His face betrayed neither shock nor annoyance. At last he said:

"I am not surprised at your conclusion. Since you are not capable of finding the murderer, you have to find somebody who would assume his guilt. It is one of the mysteries of life that the innocent are called upon to bear the guilt of the transgressors. Arrest me, if you must."

22

A soft twilight was enveloping the countryside. Jakub pulled up in a village only a few kilometers from the border. He wanted to savor his last moments in his native land. He got out of the car and walked down the village street.

It was not an attractive street. Rusty scraps and old tractor tires littered the yards. It was a neglected, ugly village. Jakub thought that the rusty junk was like a vulgar word which his native land was spitting at him by way of farewell. The street came to an end at the village green. There was a small pond in the middle of the green, and the pond was neglected, too, overgrown with algae. A few geese were splashing near the edge, and a boy was trying to shoo them out of the water with a switch.

Jakub was about to return to the car when his eye was caught by a boy standing in the window of one of the houses. The child, hardly five years old, was gazing through the windowpane toward the pond. Perhaps he was watching the geese, perhaps he was watching the boy whisking at the geese with his switch. Jakub could not tear his eyes away from his face. It was a child's face, but what fascinated Jakub were the eyeglasses. The little boy was wearing a pair of large spectacles which doubtless contained thick lenses. The boy's head was small and the glasses were huge. He was bearing them like bars, like a destiny. He was gazing through their frames as if he were looking out through the bars of a prison to which he had been given a life sentence. Jakub gazed back into the boy's eyes, and he was filled with a great sorrow.

This feeling was unexpected, like the sudden rush of water after the collapse of a dam. Jakub had not felt so sad for many, many years. He had known bitterness, disappointment, but not sorrow. And now it had suddenly burst upon him, and he could not move.

He saw the child wearing his prison, he pitied that child and his whole country; it seemed to him that he had failed his country, that he had loved it poorly, and his indifferent, unsuccessful love made him feel sad.

And then it occurred to him that it was pride that had kept him from loving his country, the pride engendered by nobility and refinement, a foolish pride that made him dislike his fellow human beings and made him hate them because he saw them only as murderers. He recalled once more that he had offered poison to a stranger, and that he was himself a murderer. He was a murderer, and his pride lay in the dust. He had become one of them, he had become a brother of all those sorry killers.

The boy with the glasses kept standing at the window like a stone statue, still gazing out toward the pond. It struck Jakub that this boy had harmed no one and yet had been condemned to the burden of a poor set of eyes for life. The thought passed through his mind that he had been blaming people for something they could not help, something born in them, something they had to bear, like an incommutable sentence. And it occurred to him that he had no exclusive claim to nobility, that the greatest nobility was in loving people even though they were murderers.

He thought of the pale blue pill, and it seemed to him that he had slipped it into the hateful nurse's medication as a message, a plea, a supplication to ordinary men to accept him even though he had always refused to be counted as one of them.

He walked briskly back to his car, opened the door, sat down behind the wheel, and began driving toward the frontier. The day before he had thought that this would be a moment of relief. That he would be glad to leave. That he would be leaving a place where he had been born by mistake, and where he didn't really belong. But now he knew that he was leaving his only homeland, and that he had no other.

23

"Don't get your hopes up," said the inspector. "Prison will not be your Calvary, we will not open its glorious gates to you. I never believed for a moment that you might be the murderer of this young woman. I only accused you to show you the absurdity of your idea that she was murdered."

"I am glad that you did not take the accusation seriously," said Bartleff in a conciliatory tone. "And you're right. It was foolish of me to attempt to win a vindication of Ruzena from you."

"I'm happy that you've settled your differences," said Dr. Skreta. "At least we have one consolation: No matter how Ruzena died, her last night on earth was beautiful."

"Look at the moon," said Bartleff, "it's shining just as brightly as yesterday, and it is turning this room into a garden. Less than twenty-four hours ago Ruzena still ruled this enchanted garden like a fairy queen."

"We really must not put so much emphasis on justice," Dr. Skreta said. "Justice is not a human thing. There is the justice of blind, cruel laws, and then perhaps there is a higher justice, but I don't understand it. I've always had the feeling that I was living *beyond justice.*"

"What do you mean?" asked Olga, surprised.

"Justice does not concern me," Dr. Skreta replied. "It is something outside and above me. In any case, it is something inhuman. I will never cooperate with this repellent power."

Olga retorted: "Are you trying to say that you recognize no universal values?"

"The values I recognize have nothing to do with justice."

"For instance?" Olga asked.

"For instance, comradeship," Dr. Skreta replied softly.

Everyone lapsed into silence, and the inspector rose to leave. At that instant a thought passed through Olga's mind. "By the way, what was the color of those pills Ruzena was carrying?" she asked.

"Pale blue," the inspector replied, adding with rekindled interest: "But why do you ask?"

Olga feared that the inspector had read her mind, and tried to make light of her question: "Oh, I just happened to see a tube of pills in her purse. I was wondering whether it was the same tube. . . ."

The inspector had not read her mind. He was tired, and bade the company good night.

After he had gone, Bartleff said to Skreta: "Our wives will be arriving soon. Shall we go to the station to meet them?"

"Let's go. Incidentally, I recommend that you take twice the usual dosage of your medication tonight," Dr. Skreta said with concern.

Bartleff disappeared into the adjoining room, and Olga said to Skreta:

"You once gave Jakub some poison. It was a pale blue pill. And he always carried it in his pocket. I know about it."

"That's absolute nonsense. I never gave him anything of the kind," Dr. Skreta replied with great firmness.

Then Bartleff returned from the other room, wearing a different necktie, and Olga took her leave of both men.

24

Bartleff and Dr. Skreta walked down the poplar-lined promenade toward the railroad station.

"Just look at that moon!" said Bartleff. "Believe me, that was really a miraculous evening and night we spent together yesterday."

"I believe you, but you shouldn't take such chances. Too much passion can be extremely dangerous for you."

Bartleff did not reply. His face radiated an expression of happy pride.

"You seem to be in an excellent mood," Dr. Skreta said.

"You're right. If I did manage to make the last night of her life a beautiful experience, then I have good reason to be happy."

"You know," Dr. Skreta said suddenly, "there is something I have long wanted to ask you and have never had the nerve to. But this day seems to have something so extraordinary about it that it gives me courage. . . ."

"By all means, Dr. Skreta, go ahead!"

"I want you to adopt me as a son."

Bartleff stopped in surprise, and Dr. Skreta proceeded to explain the reasons behind his request.

"I'd do anything in the world for you, you know that," said Bartleff. "I'm just wondering what my wife would say. It might seem foolish to her. She'd be fifteen years younger than her son. Wouldn't that pose a legal problem?"

"There is no legal stipulation that an adopted son must be younger than his parents. After all, it isn't a real son, but exactly as it says, an adopted one."

"Are you absolutely sure?"

"I settled this question with lawyers a long time ago," Dr. Skreta said with some embarrassment.

"You know, it is rather unusual and I'm somewhat taken aback," Bartleff said, "but today I am full of a special kind of elation and I want to make the whole world happy. If it really makes you happy . . . my son . . ."

The two men embraced in the middle of the street.

25

Olga was lying in bed (the radio in the neighboring room was silent). It was clear to her that Jakub had murdered Ruzena and that only she and Dr. Skreta knew it. She would probably never find out why he had done it. Her skin tingled with horror, but then she realized with surprise (we know she was good at self-observation) that the tingling was pleasant and the horror full of pride.

The previous night Jakub's mind must have contained the most terrible thoughts as she was lovingly drawing him into herself, and those thoughts therefore had become part of her.

Why doesn't this bother me? she asked herself. Why don't I denounce him to the police (and never will)? Am I, too, living beyond justice?

But as she continued her self-examination, she was increasingly filled by an odd, blissful pride. She felt like a girl who is being violated and is suddenly seized by a swooning delight, a delight which grows ever stronger the more she disapproves of it. . . .

26

The train pulled into the station and two women climbed out.

The first one looked about thirty-five and received a kiss from Dr. Skreta. The second, who was younger, stylishly dressed, and holding a child in her arms, was kissed by Bartleff.

"Let me see your little boy," said Dr. Skreta. "This is my first real look at him."

"If I didn't know you so well I would suspect you of infidelity," laughed Mrs. Skreta. "Look here, at his upper lip! He's got a birthmark in exactly the same spot as you."

Mrs. Bartleff looked carefully at Skreta's face and burst out: "It's true! I never noticed that the whole time I was here at the spa!"

Bartleff said: "It is an accident so remarkable that I feel free to describe it as a miracle. Dr. Skreta, who confers health on women, is an angel, and he leaves his angelic sign on the children he has helped bring into the world. It is therefore not an ordinary birthmark but an angelmark."

Bartleff's explanation pleased everyone and gave rise to good-natured laughter.

Bartleff turned to his attractive wife. "Besides, I hereby solemnly announce that a few minutes ago Dr. Skreta became a brother of our little John. It is therefore quite fitting that as siblings they share a common mark."

"So you have done it at last. . . ." Mrs. Skreta sighed happily.

"I don't understand. Please explain!" said Mrs. Bartleff.

"I'll tell you all about it. We have a lot to talk about today, a lot to celebrate. We've got a marvelous weekend ahead of us," said Bartleff, taking his wife by the arm. The four of them then walked to the end of the lamp-lit platform and soon left the station behind them.